CW00524794

The Haunting of Dark Angel Tunnel

CAT KNIGHT

DISCLAIMER

This story is a work of fiction, any resemblance to people is purely coincidence. All places, names, events, businesses, etc. are used in a fictional manner. All characters are from the imagination of the author.

PLEASE TAKE NOTE

The author uses British English spelling.

Prologue

Timothy sneezed and wiped his nose on the sleeve of his old coat. He asked himself for the hundredth time what he was doing in this infernal dungeon. No, it wasn't a dungeon. It was a tunnel, and it was dank and cold. It was a place to be avoided under the best of circumstances, and this was far from the best of times. Sykes was ahead of Timothy, and Sykes carried the sputtering torch, that gave off little light and less heat.

"Where we goin'?" Timothy asked for the tenth time.

"I told ya. We're goin' to a meetin'."

"In the bowels of city? What manner of man meets in such a place?"

"The manner of man that would meet with the likes of you. Now be quiet. We're almost there."

Timothy wanted to remind Sykes that he had said that a quarter of an hour ago, but Timothy didn't want to rile Sykes. Sykes was in a foul mood to begin with. Carping at him wouldn't make things better. Timothy would just have to hold his horses. Besides, Timothy wasn't certain it had been a quarter of an hour. While he considered himself a keen judge of time, it wasn't as if he had a watch or timepiece.

He wasn't of that rank. And in the bowels, he certainly couldn't hear the church bells.

Like most of those of his ilk, he depended on the chimes to tell him the time. For a moment, Timothy thought he heard the clop of horses and the clack of wheels on a cobblestone street. Then, he realised it was wishful thinking. He was too far below ground.

Of course, Timothy wasn't so keen on the meeting, to begin with. Will Tanin had the reputation of a bully and a hothead. Timothy would just as soon not meet him, especially since Timothy had been seeing Will's sister. Not that Timothy was still seeing her. He had dumped her after, well, after. He had no use of her after. He was not the marrying kind.

That was the problem in Timothy's circle. Everyone knew everyone. While he thought he had found a church outside his immediate boundary, he found out too late that the lass was kin of Will. Anne should have told him who her brothers were. In fact, she should have not been in the church at all. It was at least a mile from the imaginary line that marked the boundary of Timothy's warren. Timothy made sure of that. He wasn't about to chance upon a pure lass from his own warren.

But he had.

The only redeeming point was that no one had seen him with the lass. So, it was her word against his. He would simply claim the lass was mistaken. After all, he hadn't even used his real name. So, he told himself that whatever Will wanted, it had nothing to do with the sister Timothy had taken a few liberties with.

It wasn't his fault that she believed his pitch. Lasses should know better than to put any credence in what Timothy said. And as soon as Timothy learned she was Will's sister, well, that nixed the whole shebang. He might have stayed with her a bit longer otherwise. She was one of the more eager ones.

"How much longer?" Timothy asked.

"Hold ya water. We're almost there."

Timothy had a bad feeling about Sykes, about where they were headed. While the tunnel wasn't a sewer, it was underground, and it was damp—and cold. Timothy had always hated the cold, ever since he was a boy, and his father locked him out of the house one frigid December night. Timothy was only ten, and he wasn't quite sure what he had done to earn a night in the cold, but he got it anyway. He thought he was going to die that night, so cold he couldn't feel his toes or fingers, and it was only by the grace of God that he avoided frostbite. What he hadn't avoided was an aversion to cold. He hated it, hated it more than he could even say. And this place was cold, oh so cold.

They turned a corner and came into a large room. Like the tunnel, it was made of stone and brick. Timothy had no idea what the purpose of the room might be. In the middle of the room were two men, one of them Will Tanin, who looked mean in the torchlight. Pillars ran in two rows through the room, and along the walls were alcoves, little spaces that seemed to hold nothing at all. Timothy wondered just how they had found such a place. Sykes walked right to Will.

"Here he is," Sykes said.

"So he is," Will said. "So, he is."

To Timothy's eye, Will Tanin was all black moustache and a scar running down his cheek. Black eyes matched the moustache and gave Timothy the feeling he was looking into the eyes of Satan. No good could come from those eyes.

"Do ye know where ye are?" Will asked.

"I have no idea," Timothy answered.

"Under the city, under by a bit. The Romans built this so long ago, most people don't even know it's here."

"Why did they build it here?" Timothy asked.

"It was a cistern. They built a bunch of 'em, on account they were afraid they'd run out of water if they was sieged."

"I don't see no water," Timothy said.

"No, we don't use 'em for water anymore. We don't use 'em for nothin'. Well, every once in a while, a gang would find this place and hole up for a while. But the gang would always get found, and then, it was over."

"Why ya tellin' me all this?" Timothy asked.

"You been seein' me sister."

It wasn't a question. Will said it as a matter of fact, and that put Timothy off his game for a moment.

"You got a sister?" Timothy asked.

Will laughed, a decidedly unfriendly laugh. "Aye, and she knows ya. And ya know her."

"I don't know nothin' about your sister," Timothy said. "Ya thinkin' of someone else."

"She was in the pub Tuesday last, and she recognized ya. And if ya think we don't know that sometimes you go about as Danny Keefe, then ya must be dumber than Sykes here."

"Hey," Sykes said. "I got him here."

"I swear to ya, Will, I don't know ya sister. It's a mistake, a big mistake."

"It be a mistake, and ya made it, Timmy boy, ya made it. Ya went to church and wooed her with no intention of bein' with her. That's wrong, Timmy, very wrong."

"As sure as me sainted mother smiles down from heaven, I don't know any sister of yours. May I go straight to hell if I lie."

"Oh, ya goin' to hell all right."

Timothy knew that no matter what he said, he wasn't going to convince Will of anything. That wench, Anne, had fingered him and made sure her brother got the right rogue. So, Timothy did the only thing he could think to do. He grinned and tried to run.

He got one step before something smashed into the back of his head. His sight turned black. Timothy felt himself drop to the...cold stones.

Timothy woke in the dark. Not totally dark, but what light there was cast a bleak hue over the walls. His head pounded, and for a moment, he couldn't figure out where he was. With the throbbing headache, he thought maybe he had been tossed out of a pub. But that didn't make any sense. He tried to move, but he couldn't. In the scant light, he discovered that he stood against a wall, his arms tied in place. Tied?

He pulled his arms, but they didn't move. As his vision cleared, he found himself in some dark space. Light spilt through a tiny space toward the ceiling, not a big space, but space. That was enough for Timothy.

"HEY!" Timothy said "HEY! WHO'S OUT THERE?"

"There's the rat," Sykes said.

Timothy recognized Sykes' voice. Timothy remembered where he had been. But the cistern was big and open, not like this. Then, the truth hit Timothy like an axe. He was still in the cistern, in one of the alcoves, although this one was almost bricked up. Will's face appeared in the space.

"Timmy boy, it's good to see ya one last time. I didn't want ya to wake up on total dark and not know where ya were."

"Will, I don't know what's got into ya, but this isn't right."

Will held up a trowel laden with mortar. He slapped the mortar on the space and then slammed down a brick.

"Will," Timothy pleaded. "Ya can't do this to me. Ya can't just brick me in here."

"Oh, but I can. After what ya did to me sister, you deserve worse. Look at it this way. You'll have plenty of time to repent ya sins."

Anger shot through Timothy, an anger he wasn't sure he had. "If ye do this, I will curse you and yours till the halls of hell freeze over. DO YA HEAR ME, WILL? TILL HELL FREEZES OVER!"

Tim watched as the last brick was laid in place. For a moment, he thought maybe he could get loose.

He jerked at the ropes with all his might, but he did nothing but hurt his wrists.

"YA CURSED!" Timothy yelled. "TILL HELL FREEZES!"

Timothy banged his head against the wall, as tears ran down his cheeks. His head pounding, he knew he would die in this small, black hole.

"Till hell freezes," he wept. "Till hell freezes."

Chapter One

Lucinda unlocked the steel door and slid it to the side.

"What is this place?" Todd asked.

"An old Roman cistern," Lucinda said. "pelagus cisternis vestris, the main cistern."

"It's cold."

Lucinda wanted to tell Todd that this far below ground meant that everything was cold, well, not precisely cold, but chilly and damp. But then, that would only make him feel colder. Todd was a baby as far as comfort was concerned. Short, small, a mop of brown hair swept to one side, in some kind of 'L.A.' mode, and washed-out brown eyes. He was not the he-man Lucinda might have wanted. But he was brilliant, and the apps he created sold like ale in a pub. He had more money than he needed, and Lucinda could talk him into almost anything.

They stepped inside, and she turned on the 'lights'. The two bare bulbs that did nothing to chase the shadows out of the corners. The electricity was important, as it was something that didn't have to be added to the expense. She handed him a torch.

"I'll need this?" he asked.

"If you want to see everything," she answered.

Lucinda was Todd's 'perfect' girl, as he often told her. 'Perfect' translated into long, blonde hair, big blue eyes, a toned body that looked good in anything. Her lips might have been plumper, and her bust bigger, but she as close enough, more than close enough for Todd. That she was taller and probably stronger than Todd was overlooked by both of them. That she probably had a better all-around brain than Todd could be proved by tests. But when it came to designing and coding apps, Todd was a genius, which was fine. She was his 'perfect' woman.

She led him into the middle of the ample space, the high ceiling supported by thick columns, in straight rows. There was a row of alcoves to one side, some of them bricked up. It was mostly stone, with some brick repairs. Most people couldn't see what the cistern really was. It was Lucinda's job to help Todd see.

"Think Goth," she said. "Think dark"

"It's dark already," Todd said.

"Yes, but we're talking modern dark, strategic dark. Over there," She pointed to one end. "A bandstand. Rockers, rollers, loud and pounding. Think rave. Over there." She pointed to one side. "A bar. Neon, black light, eerie, strange. Tattoos and piercings, leather and black lipstick. Attitude and sneers. Overcoats and thick boots."

"But no smoking."

"No smoking...by law."

"And no dealing drugs?"

"Not on our watch. And over there?" She pointed. "A kitchen, nothing big. Pub food and appetizers. But it's not the food. It's the ale and the cistern, this place, so old...and cold."

"I don't like it" Todd said. "Why would anyone come here?"

"Because their friends will be here. This is a cave, Todd, a manmade cave. Of course, it's eerie. It's scary. If we do it right, that fear will bring them in. We'll give them the cave they desire, the rocky, cold cave of their dreams. Think of it. We'll corner the market for Goths, who don't have a real grotto to go to. Dark Angel will be the biggest hit this town has ever seen."

At that moment, a tiny "scree", one of the oddest sounds Lucinda had ever heard, slipped past them.

"What was that?" Todd asked.

"This cistern is almost two thousand years old. The stones rub against each other when the earth shifts. Weird, isn't it?"

"Will that happen when the Goths are here?" Todd asked.

"I hope so," she said. "It will scare the pants off them."

Todd grinned. "That will turn their black hair white."

"We'll make it happen."

"Yes, we will."

She led Todd out of the cistern, out of damp cold. She didn't have the heart to tell him that she had made up the explanation of the "scree". She had no idea where the sound had come from. And while that bothered her a little, it wasn't worth a minute of worry. Old places, like old people, made odd sounds. A logical nerd, like Todd, needed a reason.

She told herself she didn't care. If there was a weird sound or two, who cared? She would add some additional soundproofing. One little sound wouldn't stop Lucinda from running the best Goth pub in the world.

It took a week for Todd to fork over the first installment for a Goth pub. Lucinda fretted after the first three days. She thought that perhaps her 'perfection' had not been good enough. Yet, she refrained from bugging Todd. In fact, she didn't return his calls right away. She didn't want him to think he had the upper hand, although it was clear that he did. Money always trumped non-money. But at the end of the week, Lucinda got the nod and the first injection of cash. That was when she hired an architect.

The architect stood in the middle of the cistern, tablet computer in hand. Lucinda noticed that the architect, a rather hefty woman with too-short hair and too-long fingernails, ignored the click as she took notes.

"This place has so much possibility," the architect said. "It's made for scary stuff."

"Well, I'm not sure that Goth is scary, but I do want a fear vibe, a dark vibe. You can do that?"

"I can do any vibe you want. The more fear you want, the better."

Lucinda smiled, just as the "SCREE" ran past us.

"What was that?" the architect asked.

"I don't know," Lucinda admitted. "I suppose some sort of echo from the street above."

The architect raised her eyebrows. "I haven't heard any street sounds. Do I need to consider sound-deafening materials?"

"Look around," Lucinda said. "You have to consider echoes, with these hard surfaces."

"I know that, but outside sounds are different. And no matter what we do, this place will be loud, very loud."

Lucinda and the architect spent a few more minutes going through the placement of the bar, the kitchen, the bandstand, the optimal arrangement of tables and chairs and stools. The architect brought up the question of loos, and they worked out that placement too. While the cistern had electricity, plumbing was a different issue. It would require some walls to hide the piping, as Lucinda did not wish to attach the pipes to the old rock.

"You know that transforming this place into a pub is not a simple or cheap undertaking," the architect said.

"Deep pockets," Lucinda said. "My backer has deep pockets."

"He'll need them."

Lucinda stayed on after the architect left. There was something about the cistern that appealed to her, some sense of dread. She could almost see herself trapped in the place, door locked, light fading, all alone with the abject dark and the...rats.

Wait. Where were the rats?

According to highest authorities, the underground was a perfect breeding ground for rats, big rats. And yet there were no rats in the cistern, no droppings of any kind. That was unusual, wasn't it? No, it was impossible. Because there were drains in the walls, and fissures in the ceiling where the Romans pumped out the water that accumulated in the cistern. At one time, this had been a working water repository. There should be rats.

Lucinda ran her torch all about, searching for some sign of the creatures that brought the plague to Europe.

Nothing.

She smiled, shrugged, and counted her blessings. She didn't have to hire some exterminator to rid the cistern of the vile creatures. They were probably worse than the Goths. That thought made Lucinda chuckle. Of course, some Goths wanted to be worse than rats and probably were. Still, it led Lucinda to wonder if there was something about the cistern that she didn't see. What kept the rats at bay? What force made the cistern unsuitable for the rodent that had conquered the world? She took a deep breath.

"Damp, decidedly damp". Lucinda muttered to herself. And it felt colder than it had earlier. Lucinda was pretty sure that the cistern was a constant temperature. It couldn't vary much, and yet, she swore it was colder.

"What?" Lucinda asked as she turned.

She stared. Someone had said something. She could swear to that. She didn't know what was said, but someone said something. It was a voice, an unrecognizable voice. A chill ran up her spine.

She waved the torch back and forth, but she didn't find a single person. That was crazy. Someone had whispered. Yes, that was it, a whisper. Who? How? Lucinda was certain she was alone, and yet...

Then, she smiled. Of course, the ceiling vents. Sound travelled well when guided by stone, a hard surface that delivered the street voices to the cistern. She chided herself. She was acting like a scared schoolgirl. She should have expected the voices. She was surprised she didn't hear the honks and beeps and sirens that had to be above her. Silly, she was just silly. Yet, a part of her wondered, really wondered where those noises were. If a whisper could travel down a vent, why didn't other noise? She shook her head. Nothing had travelled down a vent. She had made it all up...silly, silly, silly.

She headed for the door, still waving the torch back and forth. No rats. A whisper. For a moment, she wondered if she could add the whisper to the pub. How would a person react if someone whispered in her ear? What if the cistern were haunted? Well, as far as Lucinda was concerned, it would be haunted. It was simple, really, she would create a story, a vicious, horrible story, and the victims in the story would become the voices of the pub. Dark Angel would indeed be the devil's playground. She laughed. It would be such fun to watch the Goths read the back of the menu, the story of the Roman cistern where bodies were offered to the gods.

Hhhhhhmmmmm.

Lucinda stopped in front of the closed door. Closed? She had left it open, hadn't she? Then, she remembered that the architect had left first. She had closed the door. Shaking her head, Lucinda grabbed the handle and pulled.

15

The door didn't move.

Grabbing firmly, she pulled a second time, harder. It still didn't move which seemed impossible to her. The door had never stuck before. In fact, it always slid open easily. Frowning, she jerked the door, and the door moved so fast, she lost her balance while the door crashed into the frame on the far side, the jolt echoing through her bones.

'What the HELL' she breathed.

Then she heard it. The whisper made her spin. She looked back into the cistern, expecting to find someone, anyone. Lucinda's skin prickled. Someone was in here with her. Possibly a crazy had quietly followed her in, or someone up for the lark of scaring the pants off her.

"Who are you?" Lucinda demanded her voice echoing through the cistern. "Tell me who you are."

There was no answer. Yet, the hair on her arms rose, as if affected by some form of electricity. She bit her lip. Who was out there? Who had whispered?

"You can't scare me," she called. "And you know what? I'm going to lock you in here. Put that in your pipe and smoke it. Hah!" She grabbed the door handle. "Oh, don't worry, I won't leave you in the dark for long. Just until tomorrow. Don't cry, don't get upset. I'll be back."

Lucinda stepped out and closed the door, locking it with a padlock. She felt a pang of guilt. She was locking someone in the cistern. The lights would work, so she didn't feel awful. And there weren't any rats. The someone in the cistern wouldn't have to share the space with the ugly things.

So, overall, while the stay would be cold and hard, it would not be terrifying. Besides, the person would be docile by the next day.

That night, she gave Todd an update, and he sounded gung ho. She skipped the part about locking in a cheeky stranger. That could wait till the next day. In bed, right before she fell asleep, she had the idea that perhaps there was no one in the cistern—not a live person. What if the cistern hadn't always been just a cistern? What if some bad things had happened down there? What did that mean? She fell asleep before she could answer her own questions.

Lucinda woke with her fear of the past completely forgotten. She remembered that she had to go to the cistern and set loose the person who had tried to spook her. And she thought that perhaps she should do a bit more research. Once the Romans stopped using the cistern, what happened to it? Who used it, and for what? She needed more info.

It was after lunch before Lucinda unlocked the cistern door. She had meant to get there earlier, but events precluded that. Did she feel bad? No, not a bit. People who thought scaring people was all right deserved what they received in return.

Lucinda opened the door and stared into the sheer dark of the cistern. She expected to find some mewling, sobbing miscreant. Instead, she found nothing, no one. Her first reaction was to shake, just shake.

Come in.

Chapter Two

Lucinda stared into the dark, her knees shaking. Fear, like a cold snake, coiled around her stomach. She had heard a whisper when she had expected a sob. Someone was in the cistern, and that someone should have been begging to be let out. Instead, he or she was asking Lucinda to come in. She reached inside the door and flicked on the lights, the feeble lights that turned the cistern into some sort of horror movie set. And she turned on her torch. The beam pierced the dark, but it was hardly enough.

She took one step before she stopped. It was silly to walk into the cistern by herself. What if the person inside really was some kind of psycho? She was always reading about odd, violent people who didn't mind braining someone with a tire tool or something. She needed to call a Bobby, someone with a club or gun. While it might sound bonkers to the Bobby, she would feel so much better if the police were with her.

She pulled out her phone and immediately dialed the operator. She didn't want to cause some kind of problem by dialing the emergency number. This wasn't an emergency, but it did require help. But the phone didn't work. She stared.

No service.

She was too deep underground. Her mobile didn't work, which was not just an inconvenience.

In this case, it could be dangerous. She stomped her foot in frustration. She had two choices. Lock up the cistern and find someone to join her, preferably the police. Or enter the cistern and chase out the person who was hiding behind one of the thick pillars. That was the bad part. There were many pillars, and the interloper might be behind any of them. She hefted the torch in her hand. It was enough to brain someone if she got a clean swing. That was hardly comforting, but it was the best she could do.

"All right," Lucinda called. "I'm coming in, and when I catch you, I'm going to kick your ass."

That sounded much braver than Lucinda felt. Yet, she knew what she had to do. She edged into the cistern, swinging the torch beam left and right. She watched for a flash of color or reflection, something that would tell her where the intruder was. But nothing caught the beam, which was wrong because someone had whispered.

She was especially careful around columns. She stayed away from them, making sure the backsides were clear before she moved on.

Behind you.

The whisper warned, and she spun, waving the beam all around and finding nothing.

And the whisper *laughed.*

A shudder ran up her spine. She slowly turned around, mindful of the beam, hoping to find the source of the voice. But she couldn't find it. There was nothing but the scant light and deep shadows.

Her heart beat faster as a waft of cold air rushed over her. She shivered, wondering where the draft had come from. It wasn't as if the cistern had windows or doors. There was a natural convection of some sort, but nothing COLD.

She steeled herself and started forward again. Her brain raced through possible explanations for the voice moving. And the solution was simple. The cistern was a natural amphitheater. A voice would echo all about. Someone standing at one end might well sound as if they were standing at the other. She was being stupid.

UP!

She looked up, shining the light across the ceiling. She found nothing, and she knew the voice was toying with her. She told herself to ignore the mis-directions. The owner of the voice had to lie ahead. It was that simple. The voice was meant to discourage her, transform her into a scaredy-cat. Well, she was made of sterner stuff than that. She pushed ahead, counting the number of columns between her and the far wall. Too many. She wanted to quit and go back to the door. She knew she should. Go back and find someone to join her. She edged toward the next column, biting her lip, her stomach knotted. She played the beam around the column.

Nothing.

Then, the lights winked out.

Lucinda SCREAMED.

The scream echoed through the cistern, bouncing back and forth, as if fifty women had screamed. What might be great for a Goth band was terrifying for Lucinda.

The echoes spun her about, until she became dizzy. She had to stop and close her eyes, waiting for the vertigo to dissipate, along with the voices.

Having fun?

She opened her eyes, and there in front of her stood a man. It looked like a man as the torch beam swept past.

Lucinda SCREAMED.

The echoes circled the room as she swept the beam back to the man.

What man?

Lucinda swept the light back and forth several times, but the beam failed to find the man, the short man with the unruly hair, that being about all she could remember. Where did he go?

She panned the light across the floor, thinking that the man had ducked.

No man.

She splayed the beam across the ceiling, although she didn't really believe he could be some sort of spider man that could cling to bare ceilings.

No man.

Lucinda trembled as the echoes seeped into the stones, leaving her in silence and darkness. What had happened to the lights? Except for the light from the torch, the darkness was absolute. She knew that if her torch gave out, she would be immersed in India ink, where she couldn't see her hand in front of her face.

Panic raced through Lucinda. She had always been afraid of the dark, ever since she was a little girl. She wasn't sure why she hated the dark. She supposed it was her mother's insistence that she sleep without a light, even a nightlight. Her mother was of a certain progressive persuasion that insisted on the darkest bedroom possible.

According to her mother, good sleep utterly depended on a dark room. But young girls didn't share the same persuasion. Lucinda had begged for a nightlight, only to be denied over and over. Her mother had been right about one thing. After a while, Lucinda learned to sleep in the dark—until she moved out and had her own place. Her "Angel" nightlight wasn't much, but it was enough. She slept without the fear of waking up in a thick darkness.

Lucinda's hand shook as she started toward the door. Her mind told her that she had hours of torchlight left. It hadn't even begun to fade. She could find the man in a few minutes. All she needed was some courage. But courage was in short supply. Her single goal was to escape the cistern, to get the bloody hell out of the dark room. Let the man have it—for the moment.

As soon as she found a friend to accompany her, Lucinda would be back, and she would soon rid the room of the disappearing man.

Leaving?

The whisper mocked her, but it didn't slow her. In fact, she moved more quickly until she reached the door, the closed door, the closed door that she swore had been left open. This was the second time the door had closed itself. That was proof positive that there was someone in the cistern. She gripped the handle and clenched her teeth as she jerked hard.

The door flew open, as if the hinges were oiled. It moved so fast that it left her hand and CLANGED against the stone wall. A CLANG that echoed through the cistern.

Hee, hee, hee.

Shaken, Lucinda reached for the handle. That was when she noticed that the light switch had been tripped. Someone had turned off the lights. It wasn't some electrical glitch. Someone had deliberately turned out the lights. And that meant she was not...

Alone.

For a moment, Lucinda could do nothing but stare. Then, she whirled, pointing the beam into the pitch dark of the cistern.

"I'LL BE BACK?"

Her bravado echoed off the walls.

"AND I'LL FIND YOU. HEAR ME?"

The words bounced around in a jumble that could hardly be recognized. She stepped out and closed the door, her entire body shaking. She managed to get the padlock closed on the third try, and it was only then that she felt a modicum of safety. Whoever he was, he was now locked inside, and while he could turn on the lights, that would bring scant comfort. She backed away from the door and shut off her torch. She knew she had to regroup. She knew she needed a companion. While the cistern was perfect for a Goth pub, it was hell for someone alone. She turned and hurried out, out to the light and air of the street.

Chapter Three

"What do you mean you need someone to come with?"

Todd sipped his ale and smiled, what he thought was a smile. Lucinda could have told him that the smile was woefully wanting, but she did not wish to start any kind of to-do with Todd. He was the money man, and she needed a money man.

"I need you to come with me," Lucinda said.

"Why?"

"It's complicated."

"It's complicated, or you simply don't wish to tell me the reason?"

She smiled, her second-best smile. "I was there earlier, and I believe there was someone in the cistern with me," she said.

"Impossible," Todd said immediately. "There's only one entrance, a problem we will have to address. There is no way the fire council will approve the pub unless we add at least one more exit."

"The architect is working on that," she said. "Apparently there is a tunnel that runs in the opposite direction. It was bricked up some time ago, but it should still be there. And there are narrow, winding stairs to the surface. It's not perfect, but it will suffice...with some work."

"That still says that no one can be in the cistern. And quite frankly, when I was there last, I found no hint of occupation. I don't believe anyone can be fastidious enough to pick up every bit of paper and such that comes from living."

"I understand, and I agree, but someone, a man, was inside. He switched off the lights and proceeded to scare the pants off me."

"Now, that I would pay to see," Todd said.

"Get your mind out of the gutter," she said. "Simply tell me that you'll come with me to do an inspection. If he's not there, then we have to find how he gets in and out. The last thing we need is some kind of secret passage."

"It would be like the Romans to add a secret entrance. They were quite clever, you know."

With that, Todd launched into a multi-minute description and explanation of Roman cleverness, from aqueducts to coliseums to catacombs. Lucinda sipped her ale and ate her salad and nodded at appropriate intervals. To her, Todd was the typical man. He wasn't difficult to manoeuvre.

"So, you're coming, then," she said, as he finished his history lesson.

"Of course, I'm coming," he replied. "If we can find a passage, well, that would be historical, wouldn't it? Perhaps, they would name it for me."

Lucinda might have told him that since he wasn't Roman, it wasn't likely they would name anything for him. But she was polite enough to keep that to herself.

That night, before she went to bed, Lucinda replenished her torch with fresh batteries. And she was especially thankful for her 'Angel' nightlight. The memory of the dark inside the cistern made her shiver. Pulling the covers tight to her chin Amada felt her blood run cold. There were not many things scarier than the dark unless it was a whisper in the dark; a man in the dark who wanted to play games. That was scarier than she could usually imagine.

Sleep refused to find her, so Lucinda lay awake constantly assuring herself that Todd would meet her in the morning. And, together, they would solve the mystery of the disappearing man. Perhaps, Todd was right, there just might be a passage of some sort that had been forgotten in the millennia since the cistern was built. That made sense, and if they found the passage, she would be the first to name it for Todd.

Lucinda met Todd for breakfast, which he spent almost entirely on his mobile. That didn't bother Lucinda very much, as it saved her making chitchat with him. Still, she had expected a bit more attention. She didn't get it until they reached the door to the cistern.

"Let's take a look before you unlock it," he said.

Lucinda watched as Todd tested the lock, the hasp, the hinges, the frame, everything connected with the door. In the end, he found nothing about the door that would allow someone to go in or out. Satisfied, he allowed Lucinda to unlock the door. She made sure to turn on her torch before she switched on the lights, those pathetic lights. She hesitated a moment, waiting for the whisper to greet her. But there was no whisper, no mocking, nothing.

"Shall we?" Todd asked.

She handed him a torch. "Keep it turned on."

They spent thirty minutes doing what should have been a ten-minute job. They checked all the vents and drains, all the possible ways someone might get into the cistern. They found nothing. The room was as tight as a cistern should be. Stone and brick and alcoves and damp and a bit of smell, but no other ways in or out. Todd was especially interested in the passage that would become the second way out of the pub. While it was clearly marked on the wall, the wall was clearly impassable. The bricks were solidly in place.

"I think your vagrant has moved on," Todd said as they headed for the door.

"I suppose you're right," Lucinda said. "It appears I imagined things in the dark."

"Happens all the time," Todd said. "This place has got to be as dark as a tomb without lights."

"Or darker," she said.

Todd's mobile gave a ping. Heaving an irritated worn sigh, he fossicked around for his mobile.

"Damn. Missed a meeting." He threw Lucinda a black look and rushed outside, punching at buttons.

Lucinda stood in the doorway, looking back into the cistern, Todd already out of hearing range.

Come in.

Lucinda froze, unable to move. The whisper was exactly the same as before, but she knew no one could be in the room.

She and Todd had covered every square foot. There wasn't anyone there. Not a chance. Which meant what...

She must be hearing things. That was it, she had heard things that really weren't there. Her mind had made up sounds, whispers. For some reason, for some fear, she was continuing to hear things, auditory hallucinations. Well, her mind reminded her, there was the man she had seen the day before. He wasn't auditory, was he?

She balled one hand into a fist, while her other squeezed the torch. If her mind was slipping, then, what could she know? Had she imagined it? The whisper, the cold, the man, the lights blinking out?

As if on cue, the lights flashed off. Lucinda looked at the switch, which said they were on. That meant that there had been a cut in the circuit. Did she know where the electrical box was? Because, if it did, that explained a few things about the night before. The man had cut the circuit and flipped the switch when he came into the room. That made some sense, but not a great deal, but some sort of sense. She waved the torchlight through the dark. Where was the panel box?

She hurried from the door and moved down the tunnel that led to the wide stairs. As she went, she searched for the electrical feed to the cistern. She hadn't gone far when she came to the panel box. With a smile, she tried to open it.

It didn't open. Locked. Locked?

She stared. That couldn't be. Someone had must have opened it, to kill the lights in the cistern. So, it couldn't be locked.

But it was, very locked.

Frowning, she turned from the box and hurried to the entrance to the cistern.

The weak lights had come back on.

Her brain spun for a moment. The lights had been on, and then they were off, and now they were back on again. What did that mean? She wasn't well versed in electrical circuits or breakers or fuses or whatever, still, she understood that it was probably a short, something that caused in the intermittent flow of power. That explained how the lights could be on one minute and off the next. And that short would have to be found. No, she thought, not really. The architect was configuring new wiring for the entire pub. Yet, she was pretty sure the short should be found and fixed.

Come in.

The whisper washed over like a real wave, a cold wave that penetrated her skin. The torch wavered in her hand, the light bouncing here and there. While she could explain the lights with a short, she couldn't ascribe the whisper to it. That was something else, and she needed to find out what. She wasn't yet ready to accept her own mental state. Primarily because she didn't hear whispers at home. She didn't experience the cold drafts in her car. She didn't see strange men in her bedroom. No, those events happened solely in the cistern. So, it couldn't be her brain, could it? Geographical insanity? Was that something real?

Lucinda took a deep breath and tried to calm her nerves. Did she recognise the whisper? Was it one of her friends? Did it have an accent she recognised? What about it was familiar?

Was there anything about it familiar? A rational inspection of the voice might yield something, right?

Hee, hee, hee.

She jumped back as if stung by some insect. The voice was mocking. There was no doubt about that. Was it dangerous? She wrapped an arm around herself, still holding the torch in front, shining the light into a room she was too scared to enter. She dug her nails into her side, almost relishing the pain. The pain was real, wasn't it? This wasn't some elaborate dream, wasn't it? She was truly here, feeling her mind and perhaps soul slipping over the edge, sliding inexorably into the abyss. As she stared, a shadow dashed across the room, from pillar to pillar. Quick, out of direct focus, it was a shadow, a blackness that seemed substantial and yet not really there. She stared.

Floater?

She knew her eyes held floaters, little bits of stuff that blocked her vision at times. They also cast shadows, things that seemed to be there but weren't. Was the shadow flitting across the room nothing more than a mote in her eye? That certainly seemed possible. In fact, it was probable. Wasn't it a fact, that if someone stared at an object long enough, the object moved? Only, it wasn't the object. The eye moved, which caused the image of the object to move. Humans weren't designed for staring at an object for an extended time. Humans weren't cameras. So, she had two explanations for the quick shadow— floaters and staring. Simple.

Come in.

The whisper reminded her that floaters and staring didn't explain the whisper. That would require something else.

33

That would require a visit to a psychologist, wouldn't it? And if she was going to see a psychologist, then she didn't have time for the cistern, no time at all. She needed to get her brain examined. She couldn't hang around the cistern. No, she had to go.

As she reached to flick off the light, the figure jumped from one pillar to another, and this time, Lucinda was certain that she saw something. THAT wasn't a floater. THAT wasn't due to staring. THAT was someone!

A sudden burst of courage raced through Lucinda, bringing with it a wave of sudden anger.

"STOP!" she called and ran into the room. She knew precisely what pillar the figure was hiding behind. She didn't take her eyes or her torch beam off of it. She painted the pillar with a light bullseye.

"STAY RIGHT THERE!"

She reached the pillar and paused. The last thing she wanted was to race into some sort of trap. Hadn't she seen a hundred shows where the unsuspecting person ran right into a fist or a club or a dagger or something worse? There was a lesson to be learned there. So, she stepped away from the pillar, and slowly swung around it, the light moving with her. And just before she got all the way, she jumped ahead, anxious to finally get a good look at whoever was there—although there shouldn't have been anyone there.

"GOT YOU!" The words escaped her lips as she stared at...nothing.

"NO!" she wailed. "NO!"

But it was a "no". It was a big "NO" since there was no one waiting around the pillar, which meant she had seen nothing. Nothing but something from her own imagination.

Hee, hee, hee.

The hair on her arms stood on end. A slip of cold, cold air passed over the back of her neck. She jumped and yelped, as panic raced through her brain. Something was there. She felt a touch on her arm, but when she looked, she saw nothing. A finger flipped her hair, it must have been an imaginary finger since she saw nothing. Yet, a hand grabbed her side, and she jumped away. Turning in the direction of the hand, Lucinda peered, looking, but there was nothing.

Want to play?

She backed away from the pillar, toward the door. A finger ran down her arm, making her flesh pimple.

"Oh, god," she managed to get out. "Oh, god."

Someone kissed her neck.

That was all Lucinda could take. She began to run, but she had gone only a few steps before the lights went out.

And someone grabbed her hair from behind.

Chapter Four

Lucinda jerked her head loose and sprinted for the door. The dark seemed to almost tug at her as she ran as if it were some kind of hedge. Later, she would blame her imagination. At the moment, she felt only a kind of headwind, keeping her from reaching the...door, which was slowly sliding SHUT.

Her heart leapt into her throat. She couldn't let the door close. That would leave her in the dark, with...with whoever had grabbed her hair. And she didn't have anything more lethal than a torch beam. If she was trapped...

She put on a burst of speed, turned sideways, and shot through the narrow slit. The door CLANGING shut a half-second later.

Lucinda hit the floor hard, wrenching her shoulder. She rolled away, moaning. The torch lay against a wall, its light covering her. The light wavered, split by the cracked lens of the torch. Pain arced through her back. What the bloody hell had she done? Then, as the cold from the floor seeped through her clothes, the torch went out. She almost screamed. Instead, she started to cry.

That evening, Lucinda limped into the pub.

Her shoulder still ached, and her hands were red where they had scraped on the stone. Todd had acquired a booth, and he stood as she approached.

"Lucinda?"

"Don't ask, Todd, don't ask. Is that beer for me?"

"Yes, yes, have a seat. My god, what happened?

"I fell, "she said. "We will have to treat the stone because it can be slick as bloody hell."

"I'm sure we can fix it. In a way, your falling was a kind of blessing."

"You're kidding me. You're glad I crashed?"

"No, no, nothing like that. I was just finding the silver lining in a dark cloud."

"Like hell. You found a way to avoid a heavy-duty lawsuit. Don't lie, Todd, it will make your nose grow."

"Like Giuseppe."

"Pinocchio, dummy."

"You're sure?"

"Absolutely. Stick with apps. They impress much more than your knowledge of fairy tales."

"Hey, I was just trying to help."

"You can help by giving phase one the green light."

"The architect has finished?"

"Tomorrow. But we need the quid in place. You know this."

"Consider it done." He pulled out his phone. "With this new app I can transfer the money to your account in seconds. It's one of my latest. Completely reliable and hack-proof."

"Todd, you're a genius. And by the way, we need a complete review of the sound system."

"Why's that?"

"I think there's some bleed from the street, through the vents."

"From the street? That's a long way for sound to travel."

"I was surprised too. But we have to look into it."

"Gonna bust the budget?"

"Not a chance."

"Then, do it."

The ale took the edge off Lucinda's pain, but it didn't last. By the time she was ready for bed, she was need of some serious painkillers. She had just enough ibuprofen to let her sleep four hours. After that, it was a battle until she rose to fix tea. Her body was stiff, and her shoulder didn't want to work. But she wasn't about to give in to the injury.

She had to get going. She had the architect and the contractor who would run the project meeting her at the cistern. And she would meet them. And she would give instructions. But she would be bloody well damned if she would go into the cistern alone. She was finished with that.

No more testing that "short" and the whispers. And she thought that as long as she was with someone, she was safe. She thought.

She met the contractor, an older man with a paunch and a poorly shaped white goatee. While he had never worked in a Romans cistern before, he was confident he could turn it into a first-class Goth pub in no time.

Lucinda told him that if he came in under budget and time, there'd be a bonus. The architect arrived, the plans in a big briefcase. That was when Lucinda unlocked the door and opened it. Before she reached in to turn on the lights, she listened a moment.

No whisper.

She flicked on the lights.

No man.

She smiled.

"All right," Lucinda said. "Let's get to work."

She watched them walk into the cistern. They were all going to be safe. She was certain of that.

For a while.

Chapter Five

"How is it going?" Todd asked.

Lucinda smiled across the table. The restaurant was a level up from the pub, which pleased Lucinda. Every once in a while, she enjoyed a little better food and many fewer blokes. That Todd liked the restaurant was a bonus. Todd generally didn't like all the blokes either. They made him nervous.

"It's going great," Lucinda said. "They have already made the most major changes. The new exit is open. The plumbing is will be finished soon, as will the wiring. We decided to leave the alcoves that are bricked in as they are. It will give the pub a fear factor. What do you think of putting up grave markers?"

"Grave markers?"

"You know, rest in peace and all that stuff. I think the Goths will go bonkers, like doing a rave in a kirkyard."

"Kirkyard?"

"Churchyard. You should read more."

"I don't have time. There are too many other things I need to do. Besides, no one reads anymore. It's podcasts, nothing but podcasts. I listen better than I read."

"That's bull, and you know it. But I forgive you. You like the idea of bricked up bodies?"

"No, if I thought it was true. But I don't. So, have at it." Todd sipped his wine. "Hey, can you make one of those mine?"

"Your what?"

"My grave. Put my name up there. That would be wicked cool."

"You're kidding."

"When have you known me to kid?"

Todd was correct. Lucinda had rarely seen him kid—about anything.

"I'll do it," Lucinda said. "But you know, it's sort of bad luck to put dates on your tombstone. You don't want to live up to them."

"I'm a ones and zeroes bloke. I don't believe in luck."

She shook her head. "Just because you don't believe in it doesn't mean it doesn't exist."

"Luck is why I don't gamble. If you need it to win, you're in trouble."

"Well, I believe in luck," Lucinda said. "And proper planning."

He laughed. "So, you will put my name over one of those old alcoves?"

"As you wish. But don't blame me if things don't work out. By the way, is there an end date you prefer?"

"End date?"

"For the grave marker."

Todd thought a moment. "Backdate it."

"What?"

"Make it five years ago. Five years ago on the day we open."

"You want people to think you died five years ago?"

He laughed. "Then, when I show up, they'll think I'm a ghost."

Lucinda frowned. "Now, I'm sure you're kidding."

"No, no, I'm serious. What could be better than being a ghost who's still alive? Wait, I have an even better idea. Why don't we sell the plaques?"

"Sell?"

"Sure, for a fee, anyone can have their name, dates, and epitaph of choice over the alcove."

"That's sick."

"That's Goth. They're all about death, aren't they?"

"Not predicting their own deaths."

"Why not? They'll be ghosts. After all, the place is called 'Dark Angel's', no?"

Lucinda considered the plan a moment. "I think you might have something, Todd. No wonder you create such clever apps."

"It's a way to make money, Lucinda, and I like to think I know how to do that."

"Done and done. You died five years ago; on the date of the day we open."

He laughed, but the laugh didn't make Lucinda feel better.

Although Lucinda visited the work site nearly every day, she didn't hear the whisper or see the apparition. But that didn't prove anything. There were always people about—workers, architect, contractor. She had never been alone inside the cistern. But that she hadn't experienced any visions was a good thing. It assured her that her brain was not addled. She was not suffering from some breakdown.

If she felt an occasional blast of cold air, well, that was to be expected, since they were working on the HVAC system. And there were several bouts of a rancid smell, that she attributed to the age of the cistern. After thousands of years, the place had to have some odours. She had almost forgotten about the earlier episodes, especially after the electrician assured her there were no "shorts" in her new wiring. She had reached the point where she considered being in the cistern alone.

Considered.

Her consideration went out the window when the architect called to cancel their appointment. She had come down with some bug that left her feverish and incapacitated. Lucinda was actually glad the architect was not going to infect her. The problem arose when the contractor had to beg off too. He had another project to attend to, something for a high mucky muck from the government. When he walked out of the cistern, she considered leaving with him.

Even though the room was now well-lit and silent, it still didn't feel right. Yet, she needed some pics for Todd. He was easier to handle if he got pics that displayed progress. Todd was indeed a numbers man.

Alone, Lucinda decided to make it quick. She went to the new exit, stepped into the passage and used her phone to take several pics. Then, she stepped back into the cistern and locked the exit door. While she didn't expect anyone to be walking around the tunnels, it was better to be safe than sorry. She turned toward the area where the loos were in the process of being installed.

I missed you.

Lucinda froze. The whisper was the same as before. That voice that she hadn't heard for many weeks. She bit her lip and shook. Why was this happening? She looked across the cistern. Was there a shadow behind a pillar? Was there someone waiting for her? She stared. The spot on the stone floor looked darker. That meant a shadow, didn't it? The shadow of a man? Because she was sure, it was a man. She hit her thigh with her fist. She knew she had to move, but she couldn't bring herself to do it. That shadow waited, and she knew it was evil, wrong.

"Go, just go," she told herself.

She took a step, a slow step as if wishing to simply slide by whatever waited for her. Her heart raced, and her palms felt clammy. Then, colder, as a cold draft flowed over her. The temperature in the room seemed to have dropped several degrees. Her skin turned to goose flesh. Her lip trembled. She eased through a second step, moving to the right, away from the shadow. If she could just slip past, she would reach the far door.

Did the shadow move?

She stopped again, certain that the shadow moved, that almost non-shadow.

She knew it was probably just her eyes, but what if it wasn't? What if someone was standing behind that pillar, someone with a knife. Yes, that was what waited, a bonkers killer with a knife. There would be blood, lots of blood, all of it hers. A bullet was quick, but a knife was…torture.

She slowly took another step, and the odour hit her. It was foul and dank, a smell of rotting flesh in some mouldering grave, a scent that living beings would avoid at all costs. Only carrion-eaters could stand the stench. She gagged, putting her hand over her mouth and nose, praying that she wouldn't puke all over. The stench reminded her of a rat that died in the wall of a friend's house. The smell had been awful, terrible, and her friend had wanted to open the wall and remove the carcass, but her father wouldn't allow it, insisting that the smell would dissipate over time. He was right, but for months, it seemed, the odour filled the house, the smell of death.

Her eyes watered as she stared at the shadow.

Had it moved again?

Oh, god, it had moved!

Hee, hee, hee.

Suddenly, her shoulder ached, the shoulder she had injured during her frantic dive out the door. Tears ran down her cheeks, and she didn't know if they came from the putrid air or the fear.

Move!

The order in her mind was imperative. Standing still accomplished nothing.

If she didn't move, she feared the cold would assault her and so would the smell and...whatever else the shadow wanted to throw at her.

She tried to scream, but she couldn't find her voice. She took two steps, and the momentum was a blessing. Veering to the right, she shot past a pillar. When she reached the other side, the shadow had...

Moved.

Lucinda stopped.

The shadow movement was a bad thing, a terrible thing. Staring at where the shadow used to be Lucinda sniffed back, her runny nose brought on by her streaming tears. The shadow had gone from there. Where did had it gone? She panned the space ahead of her, carefully trying to locate the shadow. It had to be there somewhere.

Where?

The man, the man she had glimpsed, was there. She had to find him. She turned, looking, doing a complete 360, checking out every pillar.

She didn't find him.

She stomped a foot, telling herself to turn again, and this time to be even slower. She had to find the shadow. She had to know where he was. Her stomach knotted as she again rotated, searching. She had to locate him, had to. She wiped her eyes, which seemed to have frozen, staring, watering. A stronger blast of cold air hit her, making her heart race. Halfway around, she spotted it...the shadow.

It was behind her, behind a pillar. The spot was darker than anywhere else, that had to be him. That had to be whatever he was or whoever he was. She bit her lip and stared a moment more. She wanted to be sure. Completely sure.

Because if that was him, then she had a clear path to the door. That was big, that was huge. If he was behind, well, then she could make it. She was sure of that. She could make it. She studied the shadow. Did it move? A wave of stench passed her, making her cough. Worse than before, she breathed through her mouth, shallow breaths, trying not to use her nose. It was awful, hideous, the stale odour of the decomposing.

Now, she told herself. Now.

She turned away from the shadow and ran for the door. She was pretty sure the man couldn't catch her. She had taken a few steps, before the lights—

Died.

Chapter Six

Lucinda faced a bad choice. She could stop or slow down and try to feel her way to the door, or she could keep running. Without a torch, she was blind, literally blind. The cistern had no ambient light. She could see nothing. She had to stop.

But she couldn't stop.

In the second she had to think, she knew that stopping would be a terrible thing, perhaps a deadly thing. She had to find the door, even if she crashed into it. Running blind was incredibly stupid, and only someone in panic mode would attempt it. Lucinda was in full panic mode. She didn't stop. She slowed a bit, right before someone grabbed her shoulder, her sore shoulder.

The hand caused her to jerk, and the jerk caused her to veer, and the veer caused her to crash.

Right into a pillar.

Lucinda's sight returned as her head hit the stone. She saw stars, lights flashing across her eyes as she collapsed. She hit the floor. The stars spun, as pain shot through her head. She stared, blinking, trying to clear her vision, her mind. Her memory seemed to disappear. Why had she been running? Why was it dark? Didn't she have the lights repaired? How in the world had she managed to crash into a pillar?

She blinked and stared, and was still, staring at the bright lights. What? What had she been doing? Before she could answer the question, the stars disappeared. Lucinda was no longer aware of anything.

She woke to blackness, to total blackness. She could see nothing at all. She placed her hand in front of her face, and her hand wasn't there. She thought perhaps she was blind. She moved her head, and pain stabbed at her, taking away her breath. She panted, telling herself to lie completely still until the pain subsided. She knew she wasn't going to move, as long as the pain was in her head.

Feeling her forehead gingerly with her fingers she found a lump that sent a pulse of pain through her head as soon as she touched it. She gasped and closed her eyes, willing the pain to disappear. It didn't, but that didn't mean anything. While she fought the pain, she tried to piece together what had happened. Her foggy mind didn't seem to want to work.

She was in the...cistern. Yes, she remembered that. She had been all alone, and the cistern was well lit. She remembered that. So, why was it black now? Wait, maybe it wasn't black. Maybe she was blind, the result of that mammoth knot on her forehead, that made sense. She was lying on the stone floor. She could feel the cold through her clothes. But why was she on the floor? Who had hit her? With what? She searched her brain.

She was in the dark. She remembered that. And she had started running, but, for the life of her, she couldn't remember why. Running in the dark? That couldn't have been the smartest thing to do. She tried to remember.

Her head ached, and she squeezed her eyes to fight the pain. Maybe remembering was not the thing to do. But she had been running, and then, she wasn't running.

Stars.

There had been stars dancing in front of her eyes, well, bright lights, so she didn't think she had always been blind. She was just blind now. From the blow to her head? She couldn't know. She was pretty sure she needed to lie still a while longer. The vicious pain would return if she tried to move. So, she blinked, her eyes watering, and tried to piece together her fractured memory slowly.

She was in the cistern, and she remembered that. She and Todd were transforming it into a Goth pub, where he wanted his death plaque placed over a bricked-up alcove. She remembered that. She thought it was akin to a death wish, but he was the money dude. What he wanted, he got. And the cistern had been transformed. New lighting had been installed. New plumbing had been installed. She had hired an architect and a contractor. She remembered that. But those were all old things. She still couldn't remember why she had been running in the dark—or running blind. It amounted to the same thing. Except running blind was probably a worse long-term outcome. She had been talking to...

The contractor.

She smiled. She remembered that. She had been waiting for the architect and talking to the contractor, and the architect had called to say she wasn't...coming. Aha, she could remember. That felt good. Her memory had not been destroyed by the lump on her forehead.

And then...the contractor had left because...because he had another job. Yes, yes, yes, that came back. She was all alone in the cistern, and that was something she had promised not to do. All alone, looking around, and she spotted the...shadow.

A ripple of fear pranced along her spine.

Yes, the shadow, the shadow of a man hiding behind a pillar. The man she had seen before, some time ago, the flash of a man, the shadow of a man. And that had scared her. She remembered that. The man behind the pillar was...evil. That was how it felt, because of the...whispers. Yes, she had heard whispers and felt cold drafts and smelled the rot of flesh. She had been frightened out of her mind. She had been afraid to move, but she had to move—because the man had moved. She remembered; she had a chance to escape. All she had to do was bolt headlong to the door. That's right, she simply had to run, and she had run. But why hadn't she reached the door?

The obvious reason dawned in her mind. She hadn't reached the door because she had crashed into a pillar. And how did she crash into a pillar? Because she was blind. Really blind? No, no, that didn't feel right. She was blind because the lights had gone out.

Yes, that was right. That explained it. No lights, running, and someone grabbed her...shoulder.

Lucinda shuddered. She had crashed because she changed directions after the man grabbed her. Which meant, she was lying on the floor, and the man was...where?

Hee, hee, hee.

Lucinda froze, not breathing. She stared, seeing nothing, that whisper racing around inside her mind. He was there, with her, and she was pretty sure he could see in the dark. He wouldn't have a problem finding her. And when he found her? She didn't want to even think about what might happen then. She needed to get out. She needed to reach the door. But her head ached, and she wasn't at all sure about her vision, and worst of all, she had no idea where the door was.

Her heart raced, and the pounding inside her head deepened. She knew she had to remain calm or try to. But she was alone in the dark of a coffin, and there was a person, a man who whispered and chased her. She wasn't sure she could move. She knew that her head was subject to spinning and vertigo. Her arms worked. But she hadn't tried her legs. With the slowness of a sloth, she raised first one leg and then the other. They both moved. And they increased her pain by only a fraction. She was feeling a bit more upbeat. She had but two problems left.

Where was the door? Where was the man?

Those were not simple problems to solve. Ideally, she would lie there until she had a good idea of the answers, but this was far from ideal. Lucinda reasoned had to move. Because there was every chance that the man knew she was now awake. That meant she didn't enjoy the luxury of time. It was time to go. She rolled to her stomach, and her head spun. For a moment, her head swam and fought nausea roiling in her stomach. Panting, she rose slowly, ever, so slowly rose to her hands and knees.

Could she walk? Not a chance.

She would have to crawl, and she had four directions to choose from. So, she needed a way to determine the proper direction.

Thinking hurt. So, Lucinda closed her eyes against the dizziness let reason come. If she ran into the pillar and fell backwards, a likely event, and since she remembered veering to the right, then, she needed to find the pillar on her right, and keep it on her right. Then, she could crawl to the far wall and move left to the door. Of course, there was the question as to why the lights had failed at all. But that was a question for another day. Right now, she had to escape, just escape. She scooted to the right, holding out a hand. It took a bit of time, but eventually, she touched a pillar. It felt like a pillar.

Come and play.

The whisper rode a cold draft that made her shiver, and the shiver made her head throb. She fought the pain and the sense of falling and crawled straight ahead. She knew that eventually, even if she went the wrong way, she would run into a wall. From there, she could find the door sooner or later. But that would take time, and she was quickly running out of energy. She was sure that in a minute or two, she would faint away. Then what? She couldn't think of that. She didn't want to come in and play, whatever that meant.

The slow pace was not admirable, but it was the best she could do. She was careful to reach out with each move, as she didn't want to run into the wall headfirst. The lump on her forehead testified to the stupidity of that.

A wave of stench rolled over her, and that was enough for Lucinda. She leaned to the side and threw up.

The vomiting made her head pound. Her entire body pulsed with pain. Her mind swirled, and she fought to stay conscious. For a minute, she didn't move, as her stomach roiled inside. This was worse than any hangover she had ever experienced. It was brutal. But after a minute, or three, she found the equilibrium to continue. And now, she would be on the lookout for the stench. She wouldn't breathe, or if she did, it would be through her mouth. She had to fight it.

She continued, hand moving out to touch anything before finding the floor. Tears came to her eyes. She felt so bad that all she wanted to do was drop to the cold stones and lie still, just give up. She wanted to.

No, no, no, no, she told herself. She was not giving up. She had to escape, no matter what.

Pushing ahead, she braced herself for the blast of frigid air. When it came, she was ready. And to her surprise, it helped. It seemed to clear her thinking. It made her shiver, and that hurt her head, but it seemed to refresh her. She felt newfound energy. She could remember—reach, plant, reach. She could focus on that. She could push the man out of her mind.

Hee, hee, hee.

She froze, as the whisper was closer, much closer, so close, she thought the speaker might be right behind her. With deliberateness that sent agony running down her spine, she looked over her shoulder. And only after she saw nothing did she realise that she had done something stupid. The room was pitch black, blacker than the bottom of the ocean. She wasn't about to see anything—unless the man possessed red eyes, like some demon.

She wanted to scold herself for being as dumb as fish without chips, but she didn't have the energy. She turned back and started again.

Reach, plant, reach.

With that mantra, Lucinda's hand soon brushed the wall. She had made it. Now, now, which way was the door. If she remembered correctly, and there was no certainty of that, the door was to her left. How far? She wasn't sure, but she needed to keep moving. She slowly turned and started along the wall, touching it occasionally to make sure she wasn't straying. In the dark, trying to keep her bearing was impossible. She needed a seeing-eye dog. No, that wouldn't do any good, because the dog wouldn't be able to see either. She needed a red-tipped cane, although she couldn't use that either, not while crawling. She had moved a few feet when her hand found the door.

Some form of joy rushed through her mind. It was the joy of a castaway who spots a ship on the horizon. She was saved. She had succeeded. Now, all she had to do was pass through the door. She was pretty sure that's all she had to do. She moved, running her hand along the door, searching for the gap. Her head pounded, but the sheer joy of finding the door kept it bearable. Her hand moved slowly, and then, it found—more rock wall.

Wait.

She knew she had left the door open. That was her rule. Had she missed the gap? No, no, not even in her current condition could she have missed the opening. She had moved from wall to wall, which meant the door was closed.

She wanted to cry harder.

She had worked so hard to make it this far, and now she couldn't get out. She was shut in. She was pretty sure the door wasn't locked, but to open it, she would need to stand. Standing was, well, not something she thought she could accomplish. Yet, she didn't have a choice. She had to try.

The stench arrived, and she pinched her nose with her fingers and panted through her mouth. Her stomach heaved, but she managed to stave off vomiting again. The effort sent waves of pain around her head, a pain that made her nauseous. A scream formed in her throat, but it didn't erupt. She couldn't waste energy on a scream. She closed her eyes until the stench disappeared. Then, she felt the door.

Lucinda thought that she could push herself to her feet, using the door as a crutch of sorts. Leaning against it, she might be able to stand, something she knew she couldn't do if she didn't have something push against. She placed her hands on the wall and struggled to get one foot under her. Then, she pushed up, using the door to help. It was working. She pulled her other foot under her and leaned against the door, panting hard. She had made it. The pain was awful, but she was standing. She reached to the side to find the handle.

Then, someone grabbed her hair.

Chapter Seven

Lucinda didn't know if it was a tug or her own lack of balance, but a moment after her hair was grabbed, she was falling away from the door. She didn't really have time to be afraid. She simply reacted, trying the best she could to grab onto the door. Something, anything would have done the trick, but the steel door was smooth, and her hands slid down, finding nothing. The only thing she could manage was to spin, falling off balance and slamming her bad shoulder into the door, sending searing pain into her neck. And while the pain was numbing, the shoulder kept her from falling backwards and perhaps giving her head another whack. She slid down the door, landing on her tush. The jarring of her spine sent stars spinning through her vision.

Don't faint, she told herself. Don't faint. Stay aware. Stay awake.

Hee, hee, hee.

"GO AWAY!" Lucinda shouted, and immediately regretted it, as agony pounded inside her head. Tears ran down her cheeks. She could only guess what she must have looked like, with a knot on her forehead and tear streaks on her cheeks and scrapes on her hands. She knew she was a mess, and the thought of worrying about that almost made her laugh.

She was battling for her life, and she was worried about her hair. Go figure.

She peered into the dark, but it did no good. She was locked in some type of tar pit, a place where sight was not an asset but a liability. Her life revolved around sight. Everything she did relied upon being able to orient herself in space defined by her eyes. But in the cistern, without light, she was disoriented. The head injury didn't help, but she was almost certain that she would be disoriented even without the injury. She wasn't made for this. No human was.

No human was.

She thought about that a second. If humans couldn't navigate in utter darkness, then what was the man chasing her? What was hee-hee-hee? Not human? That didn't make sense, and yet it did. He had proven he could find her in the dark. He could cause cold and stench. Could a human do that? It wasn't as if he could wear night-vision goggles because not even those goggles worked without some light. They were night-vision, not grave-vision. Yet, yet, he had found her. And if he wasn't human, what was he? She didn't want to answer her own question, because that was even scarier than assuming he was human. If he were something beyond humanness, did he possess powers beyond what humans possessed? Her mind and brain hurt, and the thinking wasn't getting her out of the cistern. She needed to go, to move. To wait was to…die?

With a determination she didn't know she possessed, she pushed herself up the door. Facing out, she felt with her hand, running it along the door, seeking the handle. She had no idea if she possessed the strength to open the door once she found the handle, but she would try. She had to try.

Time seemed to have slowed as if she had been in the cistern for hours, but that couldn't be right. could it? How long? Like space, time in that blackness had ceased to exist. And it didn't matter. All that mattered was getting out, was not dying.

Her hand found the handle.

A finger ran down her cheek, more terrifying than a spider.

She SCREAMED again.

Even as cold breath hit her face.

She SCREAMED again.

A finger touched her nose.

SCREAM.

And ran down her neck.

SCREAM

And touched her lips.

She spun and wrapped both hands on the handle. Then, she jerked it as hard as she could, and the door moved. It didn't open all the way, but it moved enough for her to tug herself to the opening and half fall out of the cistern. She managed to catch herself. She turned back to the door space.

The lights flicked on, and in the painful glare, she saw something, someone. Her dilated eyes couldn't stay open, and when she blinked, the something, the someone was gone.

Tears burst from her eyes, running down her cheeks. She teetered, her head reeling.

She needed hospital. She needed a bed. She backed away from the awful room. And SCREAMED when someone grabbed her.

"It's me," Todd said. "It's me."

She turned, and Todd had never looked so good.

"My god, Lucinda, what happened?"

"Hospital," she said—right before she fainted.

Chapter Eight

Lucinda woke in a hospital bed. There was a window, and it showed that night had fallen. For one frightening, tense moment, she though the window might break, and the awful dark would flood her room, shutting off all light and sound. Then, she realised she was safe, and the night couldn't push into the room and suffocate her.

"Ah, we're awake."

Lucinda turned to the voice and immediately wished she hadn't. The pain made her wince.

"Bad?" the nurse asked.

"Y...yes," Lucinda managed to answer.

"You have quite a lump on your noggin. But it's just a lump. I'll get something for your headache. By tomorrow, you should feel much better."

"No concussion?"

"Perhaps, a little, but nothing serious. You're lucky. The forehead protects better than the back of the skull."

"I don't feel so lucky."

"But you will. By the way, how did you get the lump?"

"I ran into a stone pillar."

The nurse laughed. "Playing Blind Man's Bluff?"

"No, just blind."

~ ~ ~ ~ ~

Todd picked up Lucinda the next day. While she still felt rocky, she could walk and talk and see without stars. That was something.

"What happened?" Todd asked.

Lucinda hesitated. She didn't want to tell the real story. She saw shadows and figures and heard whispers? That didn't sound right at all.

"The lights went out," Lucinda said. "I guess there's a short somewhere, or maybe the breaker tripped. I don't know. But without lights, the cistern is so black, you can't see your hand in front of your face. I was trying to find my way out when I ran into a pillar. I guess I was moving faster than I thought. Panic, you know. I don't like the dark."

"You're not the only one. Well, I was just there, and it's really coming along. It's going to be great."

"I'll take a look in a day or two. After my head stops feeling like a giant balloon."

"You've done a marvellous job, and it's on time. That's impossible in Britain these days."

"You have to stay on them all the time. But I agree, it will be the best bloody Goth pub in the world. But there a couple of details I need to clean up."

"Nothing serious, I hope."

"Nothing I can't handle."

Lucinda spent the next twenty-four hours in bed. When she climbed out, her head felt almost normal. While her head seemed all right, she knew she needed to work on whatever waited for her in the cistern. She was reasonably sure that the thing in the cistern wouldn't stop with her. Others would be plagued by the thing, the thing that cut the lights and tugged at hair. She couldn't imagine the chaos that would happen if the cistern went pitch black during a show. That would lead to a stampede, and a stampede meant a death or two.

A death would kill the pub. So, Lucinda needed to discover what it was in the cistern. And she had to do it without telling Todd, who would never believe in spirits. He would simply stop paying for the renovation. If the power couldn't be assured, there would be no pub. Simple and true.

It took two calls to her Goth friend, Laurel, to find a medium who might do a séance in the cistern. Lucinda didn't really believe in ghosts, but she was running out of options. Laurel knew several women who might be able to help, but there was no guarantee. The séance might be a bust, which would leave Lucinda exactly where she was. What did she have to lose? Not much? Would Laurel attend the séance? She would be thrilled.

Lucinda was the first to reach the cistern, and she waited outside. The last thing she needed was to be alone in that room. Looking through the doorway to the brightly lit room, Lucinda shook, and her forehead throbbed. She carried a torch because, without one, she wasn't about to enter the room. That was never going to happen again.

Laurel arrived next, and she waited outside with Lucinda. Laurel was a weekend Goth. During the week, she worked in a brokerage firm, and she was quite good at analyzing money, business, and returns. But on weekends, she donned black lipstick, black nails, black eyeliner, thick, black boots and a studded, leather jacket. Laurel was as dark as she could be. Goth raves were her weekend fare. That pudgy face and blonde hair disappeared on weekends.

Becky didn't look like a medium. Red hair, freckles, a perky smile, she seemed an imp of some kind. Short and frail, she greeted Laurel and Lucinda as if they were long-lost friends. That was not reassuring to Lucinda, who had a particular image of a medium—long dress, braids, amulets and rings everywhere. Becky wasn't like that. In fact, Becky looked like some salesperson in a toy store, or maybe one of Santa's elven helpers.

"So, this is the place," Becky said, as she looked into the room. "It is a bit different, isn't it?"

"I've had some rather harrowing experiences in there," Lucinda said.

"I should imagine so," Becky said. "There is something in there that doesn't like us. In fact, there's a malice that would like to destroy us. Do you know of anyone who was killed here?"

Laurel shook her head.

"It's been around since Roman times," Lucinda said. "I would think someone died here."

"Oh, I don't think an ordinary death would be a big problem. It's a murder that causes people to hang around. Revenge is a very powerful emotion. Everyone wants vengeance."

"I don't know of anyone specific," Lucinda said. "And I don't know of a way to find out."

"It's probably too late to determine the likely victim, but that shouldn't matter. We will see what we can learn."

Becky led the way into the cistern. She hadn't gone ten feet before a blast of frigid air hit the three.

"What the bloody hell is that?" Laurel asked.

"I'm afraid, we're not welcome," Becky said. "This may be difficult."

"I've experienced this before," Lucinda said. "Next will come an intolerable stench. I suggest you pinch your nose and breathe through your mouth."

"You're kidding," Laurel said.

"It's not uncommon," Becky said. "Angry spirits can do all sorts of nasty things."

"Kill us?" Laurel asked.

"Not likely," Becky answered. "They live for the fear."

Becky stopped in the middle of the room and looked around. "I don't like this place," she said. "Not the way it is. We need to get rid of whatever it is that is causing the problems."

At that moment, the predicted stench arrived.

While Becky and Lucinda seemed to weather the odour, Laurel started coughing and hacking. She doubled over and ended up spitting on the cold, stone floor.

"Are you all right?" Lucinda asked.

"That is the worst smell I've ever encountered," Laurel said.

"It is rather bad, isn't it," Becky observed. "But we can't let a little smell chase us out. The next wave might be worse."

"I don't see how," Laurel muttered.

Becky sank to her knees and drew a pentagram on the floor. The blue chalk seemed out of place, but Lucinda wasn't about to complain. Blue seemed better than red or…black. Becky added a circle around the pentagram and stood.

"All right," Becky said. "Before we start, let's establish some ground rules. First, I'll do the talking, unless the spirit asks to speak to one of you. Then, of course, you'll answer. We would like to get the spirit's earthly name, although getting that might be beyond our abilities. If things get really bad, we will stop."

"What do you mean by 'really bad'?" Laurel asked.

"I'm not sure, but the fear would be difficult to overcome. We would be frightened, literally, out of our minds. Panic is to be avoided."

"And if the lights go out?" Lucinda asked.

"I hope that doesn't happen because this place would be utterly dark, wouldn't it?"

"You have no idea."

"If the lights go out, we will leave. But remember, don't let go of each other's hand."

"I have a torch," Lucinda said. "We'll get out."

"You're scaring me," Laurel said.

"There's no need to be frightened," Becky said. "We'll be quite all right, I'm sure."

Lucinda was not at all sure they would be all right. In fact, she was fairly sure that they would suffer the worst the spirit could hurl their way. And she hoped that they would be able to weather the storm. She touched her temple and flinched. The memory was not one she wished to repeat.

Becky held out her hands, and the women took them, forming a circle. Lucinda felt a certain power in the threesome, although she was not at all sure there would be any significant outcome.

"We are aware of your presence," Becky began. "And we wish to come to some form of accommodation. We want to use this space. And we wish for you to move on. If you can speak, then speak now."

Hee, hee, hee.

Lucinda felt the tremble in Laurel's fingers. That was not a good sign.

"What do you want?" Becky asked. "We wish to give you what you need."

There was no answer more than a gush of cold air, which made Laurel moan.

"We mean no harm or disrespect. What is your name?"

Tim...O...thy.

"Timothy," Becky repeated. "And last name? We need your last name."

Hee, hee, hee.

"Timothy Hee?" Becky asked.

The stench rolled over them, making Laurel gag. Lucinda's eyes watered. It was awful.

"Timothy Hee," Becky said. "Why are you here? Why hasn't your spirit moved on?"

There was no answer. Lucinda felt a great dread fill her mind. She was standing on a precipice, and she knew she would soon fall into a black abyss. It was a dread she had never felt before, not even when she was in school and had to report to the headmaster. She bit her cheek, fighting the urge to scream.

"Timothy Hee," Becky said.

The lights winked out.

Total darkness reigned.

Laurel SCREAMED.

"Don't let go," Becky said.

Lucinda needed to let go of Laurel's hand. The torch wouldn't turn on itself, and with her hands occupied, Lucinda was no position to produce light.

A wind howled through the room. Laurel screamed again. Becky squeezed Lucinda's hand, and Lucinda held onto Laurel. Then, a scrap of wood (Lucinda thought it was wood) smacked Lucinda in the side.

She gasped as the foul odour swirled with the wind. This wasn't a draft, this was a whirlwind, making the experience difficult to withstand, as Lucinda's hair whipped across her face.

"Hold on," Becky said.

Laurel moaned, and Lucinda knew Laurel was unprepared for the onslaught. Another piece of wood hit Lucinda. She felt she was in the middle of a maelstrom. They needed light, but the only way to get light was to break the bond. Lucinda couldn't bring herself to let loose of the hands, not even as the wind increased, and the cold made them shiver. They were in the middle of a horrible cyclone. Lucinda could barely breathe. She knew she didn't really have a choice. She dropped their hands and reached for her torch.

Laurel SCREAMED.

"NO!" Becky yelled.

Lucinda grabbed the torch and had it on in seconds. She turned to Laurel first, where some, dark man had his hands wrapped around her neck. Lucinda froze, even as the man disappeared, and Laurel collapsed to the stone floor.

At that moment, the wind stopped. The frigid cold dissipated. The stench disappeared. Lucinda turned the light on Becky, whose sunny smile had disappeared. Her hair showed a white streak that hadn't been there before.

"We have to get out of here," Becky said. "Laurel?"

Laurel didn't answer.

Chapter Nine

"Help me," Lucinda told Becky, who seemed dazed. "HELP ME!"

Becky came alive, and the two of them grabbed Laurel. Together, they started for the door. Luckily, Lucinda's torch, with its new batteries, provided enough light.

Hee, hee, hee.

Lucinda shivered. Laurel, while conscious, seemed utterly overwhelmed. Becky didn't say a word.

"We have to get out," Lucinda said. "Otherwise, it will plague us."

If Lucinda expected an answer, she was disappointed. Becky didn't say a word. Laurel stumbled along, and while it seemed that the walk took an hour, it was only seconds before they passed through the door. As soon as they did, the lights came on. They stopped.

"Rest," Becky said.

They helped Laurel sit on the stone floor. Then, Becky sank and placed her back to the wall. Lucinda left her torch on, as she didn't trust whatever was in the cistern.

"I...I...never before," Becky managed to get out.

"I should have warned you better," Lucinda said.

"I wouldn't have believed."

"Laurel," Lucinda said. "Are you all right?"

Laurel whispered something.

"What did she say?" Lucinda asked.

"Frozen fingers, I think," Becky said.

They spent a few minutes in silence. Lucinda didn't know what to say, and the others didn't seem in any condition to add anything. It was as if their minds were working hard to process the event. Lucinda could understand. When something totally out of the ordinary occurred, the human brain needed time to place it into the memory.

"Tea," Lucinda said. "We need tea."

"And whiskey," Becky added.

Lucinda was not about to argue.

The pub was bright but mostly empty. Lucinda looked across the table to where Becky and Laurel gripped their teacups. They didn't say a word, as the barkeep delivered three shots of whiskey. Each of them grabbed a glass.

"Quick and neat," Lucinda said. "Liquid courage."

Laurel used two hands, as hers shook. Becky's glass trembled. Lucinda held hers out.

"Cheers!"

The toast sounded lame after the event in the cistern. Yet, they downed the fiery whiskey.

A polite cough was all Lucinda needed, feeling the warmth in her stomach. Even as she did, Becky held up her empty glass so the barkeep could see.

"I'm afraid one won't do," Becky said. "Laurel?"

Laurel nodded.

"Don't leave me out," Lucinda said.

It took some time, but after a bit, the tea and whiskey loosened up their vocal cords. That was when they discussed the event, an event that had left them more than a bit frightened.

"I will not go back," Laurel said. "Not until that...thing is gone."

"That's the real problem," Lucinda said. "How do we get rid of Timothy Hee...if that is his real name?"

"I believe his name is Timothy, but the 'hee' part feels wrong," Becky said.

"I don't care about a name," Laurel said. "It's wicked."

"What do we do, Becky?" Lucinda asked.

"I suspect that Timothy died in the cistern. In fact, his bones might still be there."

"How can that be?" Laurel asked. "The workers would have found them."

"The alcoves," Lucinda said. "Some have been bricked over. What if there is space behind?"

"That would make sense," Becky said. "It's what keeps the spirit there. It's what gives it power."

"How do we find them?" Lucinda asked.

"I'm not sure," Becky said. "I'm guessing that if you get close, the spirit will react in some way."

"I'm not coming," Laurel said. "Don't ask."

"I'm not sure I can take another bout with Timothy," Becky said. "Not for a while."

"First," Lucinda said. "I think I need to do a bit of research. If Timothy Hee died in the cistern, then his disappearance might be noted somewhere. What do you think? A century ago?"

"That might be a good place to start, but people come and go all the time. A disappearance might not be noticed at all," Becky said.

"I can help with the search," Laurel said. "I think I might like to know something about the man who choked me. As long as I don't have to go back in there."

"Do you, do you think he'll leave, even if we find his bones?" Lucinda asked.

"I think the bones mean a great deal," Becky said. "The spirit should follow them to the grave."

"Then, we'll look," Lucinda said.

"Don't go in there alone," Becky said.

"Not a chance," Lucinda said. "I'll have someone big and strong with me."

"You know," Becky said. "You know, you could just give it up."

"What are you saying?" Lucinda asked.

"Just give up the Goth pub, the whole idea. Seal off the cistern and let Timothy have it."

"I can't do that," Lucinda said. "Not as long as there's a chance to turn it into a pub."

"What if it doesn't work?" Laurel asked.

"That's not something I'm going to consider," Lucinda answered.

"You're braver than me," Laurel said.

"No, just a bit more stupid."

Despite the whiskey buzz, Lucinda began her search for Timothy as soon as she reached her flat. She wasn't sure where to start, as she didn't have a last name. A beginning search on "Hee" produced no results, none she could use. And there was the time frame to consider. While her glimpses of the spirit had been brief, the clothes didn't match anything in her lifetime. So, she had to pick out a period and go to work. Laurel had promised to do some looking, but Lucinda wasn't so sure Laurel would live up to her offer. Even after the whiskey, Laurel was visibly shaken by the cistern encounter. Lucinda was spooked also, but she was determined to bring the pub to life. She wasn't about to tell Todd that she was tossing all his quid into the loo. That was not acceptable, not at this stage. She needed to fight Timothy or whoever it was.

That was the real problem.

She was looking for Timothy somebody, but she wasn't at all certain the spirit really was Timothy. It might be any bloke who happened to die in the cistern, from any era. It might be a Roman, for all she knew.

Although she was pretty sure, the man didn't wear a toga—or mail, or some other time-identifying apparel.

She stayed at her computer for as long as she could, until whiskey sleepiness chased her to bed. The morning would be soon enough. Her quest would continue. As she slid under the blanket, she wondered if she possessed the wherewithal to truly rid the cistern of its ghost.

The mere thought of reentering the cistern made her shake. She was like a high-wire acrobat the day after a fall. How in the world would she dare step on the wire again? Sleep arrived before she could answer that question.

The next day was spent looking for the right Timothy. Lucinda sat in front of her computer for hours, reading list after list of possible Timothys. She had no idea that so many Timothys had disappeared through the years. While Lucinda tried to refine her search, it still returned more Timothys than she could reasonably process. Yet, she managed to winnow the information to a handful. Anyone of them might be the Timothy of the cistern.

While that helped, it didn't provide what she needed. Which Timothy (if really a Timothy) was her nemesis? She decided that one day was enough. She hadn't heard from Laurel, which was fine. Laurel had bitten off more than she could chew. She needed to recover.

While searching for Timothy had been exhausting, finding someone to join her in the cistern required finesse. Todd was out of the question. Out of the other blokes she knew, few would simply join her without some explanation. And she found it difficult to tell them that she was on a ghost hunt.

While that wouldn't have put off a few of them, it sounded like some sort of scam. No, instead of risking that, she would call the contractor she had hired. Lucinda congratulated herself on her plan. It was simple and it would serve her purpose. She would explain to the contractor that she needed to see behind one or two alcoves—for insurance purposes. While everyone agreed that there weren't any wires or pipes in the alcoves, there might be something else.

Like what? The contractor asked

Not a ghost. Although she hadn't said that. It was just that the cistern had existed through the worst plagues the world had ever known, and while the chances of a bacterium or virus surviving in an alcove was remote, it just might happen, and Lucinda was not about to be responsible for a second coming of the plague.

"Right you are then luv. We'll check it out and there'll be no question of any lethal pathogen lurking behind the bricks. We won't need to remove all the bricks, just enough to allow complete sterilization of the alcove if it's needed."

Lucinda didn't have the heart to tell him that if they found bones, they were going to remove every brick and bit of mortar. She was leaving behind no trace of Timothy Hee.

"The contractor called," Todd said from across the table. "You want to open up the alcoves?"

"Oh, I'm sorry he bothered you". Lucinda said, with her best smile. "Only it came to our attention that there might be a nasty germ or two behind the bricks. We can't take chances. So, we're going to open them enough to sterilize them."

"You can't do that without removing bricks? Don't they have some sort of x-ray or something that will kill off everything? And anyway, aren't you being a bit paranoid?"

"King Tut," Lucinda answered.

"What about King Tut?"

"When Howard Carter opened King Tut's tomb, he declared that he had set loose the curse of the Pharaohs. Those who disturbed the bones would suffer an untimely death. In fact, George Edward Stanhope Molyneux Herbert, the fifth Earl of Carnarvon, who financed the dig, actually died a year after the tomb was violated."

"So, you think there's a pharaoh buried in the cistern?"

"No, but curses come in all shapes and sizes. Some little virus, hidden away, since the time of the Romans, might hop out and infect a raft of people unprepared to battle it. Wouldn't you rather be safe than sorry?"

"I'd rather have my alcoves with their grave markers," Todd said. "But I suppose we can always put the bricks back. I'm certain we have masons who can make the mortar look two thousand years old, since they do that on a regular basis the way it is."

Lucinda laughed. "I'll see to it."

The unexpected discussion with Todd didn't turn Lucinda from her mission. She was going to battle whatever was in the cistern. And she was determined to win.

Before she actually went after Timothy, Lucinda rang up Becky. If there were any last-minute words of advice, Lucinda wanted them.

"You know what it's like," Becky said. "So, you won't be surprised."

"I'm taking two torches," Lucinda said. "And I'm going to keep one of them on all the time."

"Sounds like a good plan. And remember that once you get the bones or whatever, you have to get them out quickly, before the spirit can latch onto something else."

"Like another set of bones?"

"That would be one thing. But in a place as ancient as the cistern, there are liable to be several items that might work."

"Oh, yay, thanks for that."

"I'm trying to make this real. Finding is one thing. Removing is another."

"Do I need any sort of special bag or something?"

"No, any bag will do. But make sure to get all the bones. Leave one behind, and well, you give the spirit time and energy."

"You're a bundle of joy today," Lucinda said.

Becky laughed, and Lucinda was certain there was an element of relief in the laugh.

Becky wasn't going into the cistern. That simple fact would bring a modicum of joy to anyone.

Lucinda prepared the best she could for the ordeal. And she expected an ordeal. There wasn't much chance of getting away without some sort of confrontation. She hoped that the presence of the contractor would somehow hold Timothy at bay long enough for her to recover the bones—if there were bones. If no bones, then what? She didn't want to answer that question. She packed a big, black plastic bag into her purse and took a deep breath before heading out with two fully loaded and primed torches. She prayed they would be enough.

Lucinda arrived ten minutes early and unlocked the door. Although all the lights shone brightly, she wasn't about to enter alone. That was a mistake she wouldn't repeat. While waiting, she shoved the plastic back into the back pocket of her jeans and tested her torches for the tenth time. She was like some kind of soldier, checking her rifle over and over before battle. The torches would work. Did they possess enough firepower?

Staring into the cistern, Lucinda tried to guess which bricked-over alcove would be the one. She wanted to keep as many as possible, even if Todd put his name over one. The bricks were not the same, which meant that they had been put in place at different times. What time might be Timothy's? She couldn't tell. One guess was as good as another. She was tempted to enter the cistern and examine the alcoves, but that didn't seem prudent. Even armed with two torches, she didn't feel particularly safe.

The contractor was but a few minutes late, and he smiled, which failed to assure Lucinda.

"What are looking for?" the contractor asked.

"I'm not sure," Lucinda said. "Bones, I think."

"Bones?"

"Some believe that people might have been entombed here. And I'm not sure I want to leave the bones in place."

"Do we need some sort of approval? I mean, we wouldn't be able to move a grave without an official nod."

"At this point," she said. "I'd rather ask for forgiveness than approval, you know what I mean."

"I do indeed," he said. "This is not an official cemetery. We can say we stumbled over the bones, and well, moving them seemed like the thing to do."

"Exactly. It's amazing what one might run into while rehabbing a place."

"Then, let's be about it." He motioned at the torches. "Do you think you'll need those?"

Lucinda smiled. "I know you don't think there's a short, but you would not believe how dark it is when the lights go out."

They stepped into the cistern, and the first thing that hit them was a rush of cold air.

"That's odd," the contractor said. "We shouldn't have a draft here. I'll have to have the ventilation people take a look."

They moved along the side of the room, straight to the alcoves. There were three that were bricked in. Lucinda paused before one, wondering.

"How do we go about this?" she asked.

"I would suggest we remove a brick or two from the middle. Then, we can shine a light in, and take a look with a phone or something. If there's nothing there, we can put the bricks back."

"That makes sense," she said. "So, we may as well start with the one closest the door."

The contractor produced a hammer and chisel, and in a few minutes had removed several bricks, which he laid aside. Lucinda shined in a torch and took several photos with her phone, getting a view of everything inside. She pulled out the phone and examined the pictures.

Nothing.

No bones.

Since there were no bones, she wondered why they had bricked over the alcove to begin with. Not that it mattered. She moved to the next alcove.

"Let's see what we have here," she said.

The contractor repeated the process, removing old mortar that crumbled under the chisel and then pulling out the bricks.

"They don't make brick like this anymore," he said. "Needs a bit of care."

Lucinda didn't much care about the condition of the brick. She took more photos and found nothing. In a way, she was happy that the alcoves weren't filled with debris and animal bones.

That was what they found in the third alcove.

And it took a good half hour for the contractor to create a big enough hole for removal. But the bones were clearly not human. So, she led the way across the room to the only alcove still bricked in. As soon as the contractor raised his hammer, the stench surged over them.

"What the bloody hell is that?" the contractor asked.

"I don't know," she said. "But I've experienced it before."

"Well, we need to identify the source and rid the place of it, or you'll never open a pub down here."

The cold encased them. Lucinda could see her breath, something that told her the cold was intense.

"This can't be right," the contractor said. "Not right at all."

As the contractor removed the first brick, the lights failed. The darkness was complete except for the torch light Lucinda had kept on.

"I don't much like this," the contractor said.

"Don't stop," Lucinda said. "We don't dare stop."

Lucinda shone the light even as the contractor hammered out the mortar. The second brick came loose, and as he set it aside, she looked into the alcove. The torch flashed over a skeleton of sorts, still in clothes, staring with empty sockets back at her.

"Bloody hell," the contractor said—just before a brick hit him in the head.

Chapter Ten

Hee, hee, hee.

Lucinda shined her torch on the contractor, who lay in a heap, his head bleeding. When she heard him moan, she knew he was still alive, although that might not be the case in minute or two. She needed to finish the job. She needed to remove the bones, as she was now certain she had found the correct alcove. She reached down and plucked up the hammer, even as a brick sailed past her head and slammed into the wall.

"NO!" Lucinda yelled as she held the torch on the hole. "YOU'RE COMING OUT!"

The stench and cold wrapped around her, and for a moment, she wavered, not at all sure she could remain conscious. Still, she swung and hit the wall of brick, and while she didn't open the hole wider, she did manage to dislodge a brick. Another swing and the brick fell into the alcove, which was fine with her. She reached back to swing again, and a brick struck her shoulder. The hammer dropped from her hand, and she SCREAMED.

HEE, HEE, HEE

For a moment, she couldn't decide what to do. She was certain she had to keep opening the alcove, but at the same time, she had to dodge bricks she couldn't see coming.

The dark was complete. She walked her torchlight across the floor until she came to the hammer. Her shoulder throbbed as she grabbed the tool. With a newfound energy she smashed another brick into the alcove.

She stepped to the side as a brick missed her and hit the wall. That almost made her smile, but she was a long way from smiling as she stepped back and smashed a brick.

Lucinda screamed as a brick hurled towards her, stepping smoothly aside it landed with a THUNK.

"You bastard, I'm NOT dead yet, but YOU ARE. Why don't you just get the hell out of here? I'm not going anywhere."

Swinging the hammer hard she knocked out another brick and dodged as a brick flashed past.

"ARRRGH. Oh God." A second brick came flying and smashed into Lucinda's arm, and she yelled again as the torch went clattering.

With dead fingers, she grabbed the torch and shone it through the hole.

"I'm coming for you," she forced through clenched lips.

Come and play.

She swung wildly, as hard as she could, and two bricks fell away. She was making progress, despite the waves of cold and stench that rolled over her. But her strength was flagging. She wasn't a construction worker. She wasn't prepared for this. Yet, she didn't dare stop. Whatever force was in the cistern would surely drive her to her knees if she stopped.

Two more bricks fell into the alcove.

A brick crashed just inches from her head.

Panting, she shined the light inside, and she spotted the ropes that tied the skeleton to the wall. The ropes were old and weak, but that didn't mean the skeleton would be easy to remove. She smashed another brick and stepped to the side. She was not certain that the hole was big enough for her to crawl through. Once inside, she hoped she would be able to dislodge the skeleton. Torch in one hand, hammer in the other, she slipped into the alcove and faced the hideous skeleton.

For more seconds than she thought possible, Lucinda could do nothing but stare at the bones, the old clothes, the ropes. She could imagine what it must have been like to watch the bricks being placed, the dark growing from a puddle around her feet to a pond around her waist, until she was completely drowned in the inkiness.

She could imagine the screams and tears, the awful minutes that turned into hours and days, the inevitable pain of coming death. The death had to be horrible, something straight from a medieval tale. She stared, imagining, shaking, too afraid to touch the bones. It was as if she were feeling something horribly infectious and deadly.

Afraid? Hee, hee, hee.

"NO!"

Lucinda grabbed the rope around one bony wrist and tugged. The rotten rope broke easily, and she cast it aside, as the wrist swung out and slapped her shoulder.

SCREAM.

The touch of the bone burned her somehow, almost paralyzing her arm. Yet, she couldn't stop, not now. She reached out and jerked the other rope. This time, when the wrist swung, she managed to avoid it. She dropped to a knee among the loose bricks and pulled loose one ankle. As quickly as possible, she pulled loose the other ankle, and the skeleton fell off the wall. Behind her, the brick wall...collapsed.

Heavy bricks covered her leg, as mortar dust filled the air. She sucked in a mouthful of dust and coughed, hacking, even as she tried to extricate her leg from the pile. The cold and stench filled the alcove, which made her cough harder. Tears ran down her cheeks. For a moment, she wanted nothing more than for the assaults to cease. She just wanted to get away. But she was no longer certain that would be allowed. In some crude way, the ghost was trying to entomb her in the alcove.

She freed her leg from the pile of bricks and discovered that her torchlight was dimming.

"Noooooooooo." She said and looked around. She knew that once the torch began to dim, it would die quickly, and she could ill afford to be cast into the darkness of the cistern. If that happened, she would never escape with the spirit on the attack. So Lucinda did the only thing she could think to do, and grabbed the skeleton and hurled it over the pile of bricks and onto the cistern floor.

NOOOOOOOOOOOOOO

Aching, panting, sobbing, coughing, Lucinda crawled over the brick pile, scraping her hands and praying that the torch beam would last. Abandoning the contractor, she grabbed the coat of the skeleton, only to have it rip apart at first tug.

Fighting the panic rising up her throat, she pulled and pulled, but couldn't move the frame out. She would have to carry it. Lucinda felt nausea threaten her. She could hardly bring herself to consider such an act, let alone execute it. Staring at the skeleton and the clothes and the fading light, Lucinda knew, she had no choice, and there was no time to deliberate.

Hee, hee, hee

Urgency prodded her. She dropped to one knee, the sore knee, and scooped up the skeleton. The bones seemed to burn her skin, but it didn't stop her. Standing and with more speed than she thought herself capable of, she fairly ran to the open door. It held still as she crossed through it, as happy and giddy as she could be. She dropped the bones and waited for the lights.

They had to come on, didn't they? She had the bones out. She had ripped out the ghost and the power. Where were the lights? They had to come on. Where. Were. They?

She ran the torch over the bones, and that was when she noticed it, noticed what had to be the answer.

The skeleton was missing a shoe, and with the shoe would be a foot, and the foot would have bones, bones that gave the spirit its power, its hate. And that shoe, those bones were still in the

Cistern.

Lucinda shone the torchlight into the cistern and shook like a leaf in a stiff wind. How could she go back in? She wanted to finish this, but how could she go back?

But she didn't have any choice. The contractor was still in the dark, and she supposed that abandoning him would prove fatal. She stared at the fading torch and wondered where she had lost the backup. Probably in the alcove, which made it useless. Fighting the shivers, she ran into the darkness.

She moved as fast as she could, waving the light back and forth and praying that the shoe would soon appear.

Hee, hee, hee

The light flicked over the shoe, filled with white bones. Lucinda trained the faint, yellow halo on the shoe and limped to it. She grabbed the shoe and spun toward the door, which was lost in the dark.

Hee

The light faded as she ran as fast as her body allowed.

Hee

She told herself she would make it. But deep inside, she knew she wouldn't. The door was too far, the light too dim. She wanted to cry, but she couldn't cry.

Hee

She flipped up the light, and ahead was the door, at the very end of the yellow cone of light.

Too far.

She SCREAMED and did the only thing she could think to do. She hurled the shoe at the open space.

She never saw the shoe pass out the door. The flashlight died, and she stopped.

HEEEEEEEEEEEEEEEE

Lucinda closed her eyes, readying for the onslaught.

Nothing happened.

She opened her eyes.

The lights were on. She looked ahead.

Through the door, lying on its side, was the shoe. As she watched, a single bone fell out. It took two rolls toward the cistern before it stopped and quivered.

Lucinda limped, dragging her foot. She crossed the threshold and kicked the bone as far as she could.

Epilogue

Black lights cast an eerie, purple light over the bar, the stools filled with Goths of every age and description. While the majority consisted of the young and the hungry, a number of elder men and women, or just people in black filled the tables. While Lucinda was not part of the culture, she recognized the badges the Goth people wore. She stood at the end of the bar and watched, as the band worked through its setup. A month since the opening, Dark Angel's had become known for the best in Goth music, with bands coming from all over Europe. Lucinda had seen to the sound-deadening material attached to the stone in places, the cistern still echoed with an incredible reverberation. Late at night, when the band was pounding, the lights dimmed, the spots playing back and forth, the Goth crowd became a kind of being, a mass roiling and twisting to the thumps of the music. That never ceased to please and excite Lucinda.

"We are going to rock tonight," Laurel said as she slid up to Lucinda.

"The crowd looks lively," Lucinda said and laughed.

"And that doesn't happen often in the Goth community."

"You're over it all, aren't you?" Lucinda asked.

"Just don't turn out the lights."

"Not ever again. I promise."

Laurel kissed Lucinda on the cheek and moved off. Lucinda didn't move as Todd sidled up, still short and smiling. Lucinda guessed Todd was adding up the numbers inside his head, how many people at how much per person. Todd always followed his investments.

"I'm glad you talked me into this," he said. It's rather perfect for a Goth venue."

"When the band starts up, it's going to be so loud, you won't hear yourself think," she said.

"Fine with me. I've been thinking too much lately. Hey, has anyone said anything about my grave marker?"

Lucinda glanced over at the bricked-up alcove, the one that, at one time, held the bones of Timothy Somebody. She had decided it would fit Todd's style, and it just might scare off Timothy, should he wish to take over the alcove a second time. So far, the cistern hadn't suffered a re-infestation.

"As a matter of fact," Lucinda said. "Several people have asked if the marker is real. Is dear old Todd really buried there?"

"What did you tell them?"

"I told them the Todd's bones were just behind those bricks, just waiting for someone to dig them out."

He grinned. "That's boffo, wonderful. I like the idea that I will be here for a long, long time."

With that, Todd moved off, ostensibly to look at his marker. Lucinda wanted to laugh. People loved seeing things about themselves. It was just a different sort of selfie.

At that moment, the ban struck a chord that echoed through the room. The patrons stood and cheered. The show was about to begin.

Lucinda listened closely. Could she hear a *hee, hee, hee*?

No, nothing.

She smiled.

The End

I hope that you enjoyed this book.

If you are willing to leave a short and honest review for me on Amazon, it will be very much appreciated, as reviews help to get my books noticed.

Over the page you will find a preview of one of my other books,

The Haunting of Hemlock Grove Manor

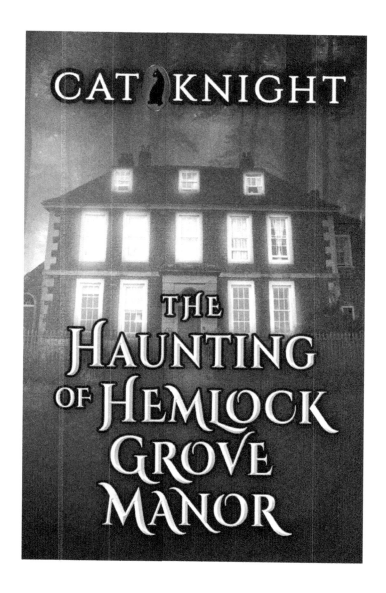

PREVIEW

The Haunting of Hemlock Grove Manor

CAT KNIGHT

Chapter One

Sometimes the world was so loud it was impossible for Mikala to hear her own thoughts. That's how she felt trying to find sleep tucked between the horns blaring on the street nine stories below, and the boisterous neighbours surrounding the shoebox apartment. Slumber never came immediately; it took time, and often with the aid of earplugs. If Mikala slept in on the weekends occasionally she'd use over-the-counter sleep aids. Eventually, the cacophony of the city spilled into her ears or rustled her from medicated snoozing.

The pulse of the city sometimes infected Mikala's dreams. Neighbours yelling through paper-thin walls, vehicles with rusted mufflers and the racket that seeped into her thoughts, spoiling tranquil bliss with urban poison. Every day the miasmic leached into her apartment with its tapestry of machines and people working in total disharmony.

Nine floors above the busy street, in a city that never learned to sleep at night, Mikala heard everything. Shouting, laughing, people conversing with other people, some people arguing out loud with themselves.

Mikala lived in the cramped apartment for the past three years, ever since she took the job. She knew her neighbours by face but not names.

She learned more those that lived closest to her apartment not because of interaction, but because of hearing them through the uninsulated walls.

The congested apartment building had a collection of tenants that never used their 'indoor' voices. The old man to the right of her was hard of hearing and the volume on the television remained loud all the time. He watched the same cable news network day and night, while she didn't own a TV. But she was polite, smiled, and went about her business.

"Mikala," a voice called. She opened her eyes, peering around at the studio, lying on her stomach in bed. She was alone in the apartment.

Did she share a name with someone else in the building? Mikala wondered. Or was someone calling her name from the dream again? She rolled over, staring at the cracks in the plaster of the ceiling and lay still listening.

The roar of traffic on the city streets came through the closed window. It was 4:28 am. Commuters got a head start for the highways. In the apartment above her, heavy foot traffic told Mikala her neighbours were awake, and their voices began to clash. She knew rudimentary Spanish, but not enough to follow the conversation.

It was the dream again; she surmised with a sigh. The voice called her from far away. It was barely audible over the metropolis clamour.

The reoccurring dream managed to find Mikala when she descended into exhaustive sleep — slipping harmoniously into the subconscious world. The voice called to her from the lonely folds of darkness.

How long had she heard that voice?

How long had she dreamed the same dream over and over, like the unchanged advertisements on the neighbour's TV during the news programs?

Strangely, the voice in the night, calling from her dreams, gave Mikala a sense of purpose, even peace. Someone wanted her, needed her for something more than what she found in her daily life. Even if it was a fantasy, at least, Mikala thought with some solace, someone needed her to fill their loneliness.

Chapter Two

The adjunct professor position at the city campus was nothing more than a glorified substitute teaching job. Since she had no seniority, no tenure prospect, and sat on the very bottom rung of the faculty, Mikala taught first-year students. Most were brand new to college and didn't give classes their full attention. Most of the students had no consideration or awareness in Mikala 's classes. It was as if they had a collective loss of interest and intellect the moment they started college.

Since it was a few weeks from spring finals, the few students who wanted better grade averages took a class period to study. The majority barely had passing grades. When Mikala scanned the latest crop of undergraduates, she felt the abject distance from the class. Most of the students used laptops and smartphones to look up anthropology assignments, gathering the first few search results to cull papers together without source citing. Most textbooks brought to class, if students purchased them, still had crisp pages and new spines.

But Cultural Anthropology was a subject Mikala loved passionately and, despite the lack lustre of many of her students, Mikala enjoyed teaching. She appreciated the 'professor' status she'd earned.

Yet since her academic career had started as an adjunct professor at a two-year college, and hadn't progressed Mikala felt that's where her academia stalled.

Three years later, it felt like she'd wasted energy striving to get her a seat at the faculty table.

There were no tenure options. With no clout or rank, and most long-term professors ignored Mikala .

"Hey, what's up?" it came as a greeting, of sorts.

Mikala looked up from scanning emails. The young man standing in front of her desk had a glazed look and slack jaw.

She did her best to smile. "What can I do for you, Mr. Davis?" Mikala kept her interactions with students on a professional level. She was ten years Jacob's senior, at least. Nonetheless, addressing him by his surname held the fissure between student and professor.

"So, you're like a doctor, right?"

Mikala sighed. "Not exactly," she said. She'd had that conversation before with other students. They didn't talk to each other, she noticed. Most conversations students had while in class either happened at the beginning or during lectures when they were talking to their laps. Mikala assumed that's where most of them kept the smartphones, out of sight.

"So, you know if I'm gonna pass the class this year?"

She wasn't sure if it was a question or statement. Mikala pursed her lips and squinted at Davis. Grades were posted online every weekend, he had access, like everyone else. Somehow, she felt there was more to the conversation topic than she understood.

"I believe you'll squeak by Mr. Davis."

He nodded. There was effort enough for half a smile returned.

He hovered, impulsively playing with the miniature plastic globe near his hand. Mikala realized he wasn't going away.

"Is there something else I can do for you, Mr. Davis?"

"Um, yeah," he said, and then immediately lowered his voice. "You want to go out sometime?"

She took it as a joke. It was a joke, wasn't it? It wasn't Mikala's intention to embarrass Jacob Davis. He looked crushed as he moved away from her desk because she laughed so hard, everyone stopped texting, expecting to see something humorous. Instead, everyone saw the young man slink away from the front of the lecture hall. He exited class without delay before the session ended.

Unable to feel disheartened by embarrassing the freshman student, Mikala went back to scanning emails. That's when her heart fluttered. Mikala received a promising email from the Dean of Hemlock Grove University in New Hampshire. She'd applied to several colleges during fall break. Single and young, Mikala wasn't committed to the city college if they used her as a doorstop for incoming students.

She wanted something important, something prestigious. It was a long-shot considering she was thirty-six, single, and not afraid to settle for something slightly above the adjunct professor. And now the Dean of Hemlock Grove University wanted a face to face interview with her.

With term ending soon and a seven-hour drive to look forward to, Mikala felt her career path was about to change.

READ THE REST HERE

HERE ARE SOME OF MY OTHER BOOKS

The British Hauntings Series

The Haunting of Elleric Lodge - http://a-fwd.to/6aa9u0N

The Haunting of Fairview House - http://a-fwd.to/6lKwbG1

The Haunting of Weaver House - http://a-fwd.to/7Do5KDi

The Haunting of Grayson House - http://a-fwd.to/3nu8fqk

The Haunting of Keira O'Connell - http://a-fwd.to/2qrTERv

The Haunting of Ferncoombe Manor http://a-fwd.to/32MzXfz

The Haunting of Highcliff Hall - http://a-fwd.to/2Fsd7F6

The Haunting of Harrow House - http://a-fwd.to/aQkzLPf

The Haunting of Stone Street Cemetery http://a-fwd.to/1txL6vk

The Haunting of Rochford House http://a-fwd.to/6hbXYp0

The Haunting of Knoll House http://a-fwd.to/1GC9MrD

The Haunting of the Grey Lady http://a-fwd.to/4EUSjb7

The Haunting of Blakely Manor http://a-fwd.to/3b2B631

The Yuletide Haunting http://a-fwd.to/7a5QF4S

The Haunting of Fort Recluse http://a-fwd.to/3Hz77lX

The Haunting Trap http://a-fwd.to/5hw7zJ8

The Haunting of Montgomery House http://a-fwd.to/20ia6sP

The Haunting of Mackenzie Keep http://a-fwd.to/7n2AWxp

The Haunting of Gatesworld Manor http://a-fwd.to/3XlZUEK

The Haunting of The Lost Traveller Tavern http://a-fwd.to/3GAG1nG

The Haunting of the House on the Hill http://a-fwd.to/1X2Wtcn

The Haunting of Hemlock Grove Manor http://a-fwd.to/LpE0k9j

Ghosts and Haunted Houses: a British Hauntings Collection – http://a-fwd.to/58aWoW8

The Ghost Sight Chronicles

The Haunting on the Ridgeway - http://a-fwd.to/1bGBJ6O

Cursed to Haunt - http://a-fwd.to/7BiHzLj

The Revenge Haunting. http://a-fwd.to/67V0NBO

About the Author

Cat Knight has been fascinated by fantasy and the paranormal since she was a child. Where others saw animals in clouds, Cat saw giants and spirits. A mossy rock was home to faeries, and laying beneath the earth another dimension existed.

That was during the day.

By night there were evil spirits lurking in the closet and under her bed. They whirled around her in the witching hour, daring her to come out from under her blanket and face them. She breathed in a whisper and never poked her head out from under her covers nor got up in the dark no matter how scared she was, because for sure, she would die at the hands of ghosts or demons.

How she ever grew up without suffocating remains a mystery.

RECEIVE THE HAUNTING OF LILAC HOUSE FREE!

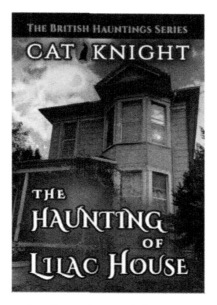

When you subscribe to Cat Knight's newsletter for new release announcements

SUBSCRIBE HERE

Like me on Facebook

Printed in Great Britain
by Amazon